A
Death
for
Adonis

A Death for Adonis

E. X. Giroux

St. Martin's Press
New York

Design by Manuela Paul

Library of Congress Cataloging in Publication Data

Shannon, Doris.
    A death for Adonis.

    I. Title.
PR9199.3.S49D4   1984   813'.54   83–24460
ISBN 0–312–18610–X

10 9 8 7 6 5 4 3 2

This book is for Russell Gordon Paterson.

CHAPTER I

The words that had been spoken had no place in the tranquil room. Sunlight filtered through floor-length windows, settling in a pool on a fine Aubusson carpet and leaving the book-lined walls shadowed and indistinct. The man sat with his back to the windows. The woman faced him across the expanse of his polished desk. Neither looked directly at the other. He appeared engrossed in a slim sheaf of papers neatly arranged on the green blotter. The woman steadily watched the toe of her shoe tracing a pattern on the dim colors of the rug. Almost tangibly between them hovered the words, alien, infinitely distasteful, and faintly frightening.

Finally the man moved, pushing the papers away from him. The woman's eyes, brilliant and lizardlike, darted from her shoes and brushed across his face. He hesitated, as though groping among the words for one he wished to isolate.

"This murder and the rest of it . . . how long ago did it all happen?"

"Twenty-five years ago. At least," she hesitated, "in two weeks, twenty-five years."

"That would make it August twenty-fifth, 1944."

She didn't speak. Her eyes were busy with the tip of her shoe again. He waited a moment and then continued, "The accused was tried, found guilty, and sentenced. Now you wish the case to be investigated and if new evidence is found you hope to reopen the whole affair. Is that correct, Miss Pennell?"

"That is correct." This time she lifted her head and their eyes met. "Please don't call me Miss, it sounds so cold. I prefer Elizabeth."

"Very well, Elizabeth. To be blunt I can't see anything to be gained by an investigation. In the first place I no longer practice law and I am certainly not what you Americans call a private eye." Glancing down, he flicked one of the papers with a finger. "I assume the lady who recommended me mentioned both these facts."

Her lips quivered and she smiled, her eyes traveling from his slenderly elegant figure to the window and the sweep of turf that ended at the banks of a placid pool. "Amelia didn't accuse you of being a private eye." Her smile vanished. "She merely said that you had been an enormous help to her in a highly private matter and that you might consent to help me. As I told you, the accused as you call him is my father and I must find out once and for all whether there is any possibility of his innocence. This may sound dramatic, but the balance of my life, or perhaps I should say normal life, depends on it. You see, Mr. Forsythe . . ." she hesitated.

"Robert," he offered in answer to the question in her eyes.

She accepted it. "Robert. I might be able to live with the knowledge that in the heat of anger my father could kill, but this butchery—"

Forsythe interrupted. His expression was gentler and his manner a trifle less formal. "The second point I was going to make was that it is not likely after this length of time that any new evidence can be uncovered. But we'll leave that for the moment. Do you mind telling me when you heard about your background? Your uncle adopted you, changed your last name. Did he conceal the crime your father was convicted of from you?"

She shook her head. "No, he never tried. My mother died when I was born. By the time I was three months old my aunt and uncle were homeward bound with me to Boston. When I was old enough to understand, about seven I suppose, Uncle Howard told me that my aunt and he were not my parents. When I was twelve he told me some facts about my parents. That was the first time I knew that Sebastian Calvert was my father. I was told that he was a convicted murderer. I was also told my father didn't receive the death penalty for his crime, but is still alive if you can call being catatonic living. My uncle wanted me to hear that from him, not from someone else. But the actual details, I guess the newspapers would call them the gory details, I didn't learn until I was sixteen."

She shot a look at Forsythe, her eyes penetrating. "I think I know what you're driving at. My adopted parents died at the same time, an automobile accident, when I was twenty-two. I inherited a sizable estate. I'm also in control of two separate businesses, an interior decorating firm and a women's clothing factory. All the Calverts are talented people. I am too. I'm an excellent clothing designer. That's what you want to know, isn't it?"

"You're very direct. Yes, that's it. You were well aware of your heritage; you had plenty of money to investigate it. You also mentioned that you were six at the time of your father's trial, which would place you over thirty now. For almost a decade you could have acted but didn't. Why now?"

Fumbling in her purse, Elizabeth Pennell found a cigarette case and removed a gold-tipped tube. Forsythe rose and moved around the desk. He offered her his lighter and then perched on the corner of the desk.

Exhaling gray smoke, she gazed up at him. "From the

time I was very young my life was conditioned, I suppose by
me. I learned to accept the fact that I am Sebastian Calvert's
daughter. I never learned to accept the fact that he'd killed the
way they said he had. How was it put? Oh yes, 'the most brutal,
bizarre, and perverted in England's bloody history'—"

Forsythe broke in. "He is also considered one of England's foremost artists."

She brushed this aside as though it was of no conse-
quence. "Save your platitudes, Robert. Quite frankly I don't
give a damn about his work. Don't expect me to be a dutiful
daughter pretending and mouthing dutiful remarks about him.
My father had time to raise my cousin Rosemary; he had time
to remarry; but he had no time for me. He didn't want me; my
mother's brother could have me. Fine, I'm interested in me too.
My whole life has been built around my father's actions. No life
for Elizabeth. She had her work and her friends. She even had
a number of casual sexual affairs."

Breaking off, the woman looked up at Forsythe. His face
was expressionless. She reached past him and snubbed her cigarette in an ashtray.

"I may sound cold and hard, but it's the truth. I could
never trust myself to have any real intimacy, not after what
happened to my father's love. Emotion was forbidden to me.
Then a few months ago I fell hopelessly, madly, passionately in
love. I use these adjectives deliberately. The daughter of Sebastian Calvert can't afford to indulge herself this way. Think
where his madness and passion is supposed to have led."

Breaking off, she sat silently for a minute, one hand
pleating the soft silk of her dress. The hand was large for her
size, almost ugly with powerful, spatulate fingers.

Forsythe regarded her closely. He admitted wryly to
himself that his first impression of Elizabeth Pennell had vanished like most first impressions into limbo. When she had
entered his study, one hand extended to him, the other grasping
the letter of introduction, he had seen a small compact woman

with magnificent dark eyes, a slightly sallow complexion, and a large nose. The eyes remained magnificent but now the nose was revealed as perfect for her features, thin, high-bridged, and arrogant. He sensed behind her composure, conflict and a tightly leashed power. She disturbed him, filled him with a sense of unease. Reaching for his pipe, he started to fill it, patiently waiting for her to continue.

As though suddenly noticing what her hand was doing, she stopped her nervous pleating and folded both hands quietly in her lap.

"So you see why I feel I must do *something*. All I ask of you is to give it a try. If you're unsuccessful, I'll have to give up this attachment. But if you do turn up something that points to my father's innocence, I will feel free to live as others live, to love as others love."

It was her turn to wait. He returned to his leather chair behind the desk and sank into it. "You've been most candid; now it appears to be my turn. There are many excellent investigators in England. I can recommend several. I'm afraid, Elizabeth, that I'm the very worse choice you could have made to deal with this matter. My own past—"

"I know about your past." Her voice was low-pitched but forceful. "One of these investigators you are so fond of mentioning got the full rundown on it for me. I'm not a babe in the woods. I happen to be a hardheaded businesswoman. I know all about Robert Forsythe, barrister from a long line of barristers, something of a child prodigy, passed the bar exams at an extremely early age and started to make good predictions of a brilliant career, gave up said career suddenly in his twenty-seventh year and returned to the family home in Sussex, where he has lived as something of a recluse for six years."

Forsythe kept his face impassive. "Then you know the reason why the so-called brilliant career was given up, why I voluntarily retired from my practice."

A small smile drew her heavy brows together. "Yes, at

least I know the rumors. Reportedly, you got out just before the legal profession could start disbarring actions." Her eyes flicked quickly toward his face again. "And I have heard about Virginia Telser."

He couldn't keep the bitterness out of his voice. "After this, you still wish to engage me, a barrister who betrayed his profession and banished himself to avoid a charge of misconduct?"

Her voice was lower. He had to strain to hear her. "Possibly that was what decided me. You are a pariah too. I don't know whether you're innocent or guilty, but you live in the shadows, watching life. I thought you might be able to understand how I feel, why this is so important to me." Her eyes didn't flick toward his face this time; she caught his eyes and held them steadily, relentlessly. "Are you afraid?"

He didn't flinch. "Of course I'm afraid. I'd be a fool not to be. If I do undertake this dredging into the past, a nasty case at the time and swelled into a monstrous legend now, I'll be forced to come into contact with, to interview some of the very people I've been more or less avoiding."

Her eyes were still locked with his. "Will you do it?"

If she had shown any signs of weakness, any tears, any pleading, he might have been able to have given her a flat no. She didn't. Her eyes contained only a challenge and a hint of derision. The gauntlet was in front of him. He picked it up.

"Where can I contact you?"

She named an address in London. "I've taken a small service flat. About your fee . . ."

It was his opportunity to throw the derision back at her. "We'll discuss money later. If I'm lucky, you may name your own amount. If not, I'll present a bill for expenses."

Rising briskly, she smoothed the dark silk over her hips. Forsythe was on his feet, his finger pressing the button on the edge of his desk.

The door swung open and Miss Sanderson appeared. She arched her brows inquiringly at him.

"Please show Miss Pennell out. Good day, Elizabeth."

Throwing him a cool smile, she followed his secretary's spare figure into the hall. Forsythe had one final glimpse of her as the door closed. Turning, he flung open the long window behind him and leaned against the frame, gazing unseeingly down the green slope to the waters of the pool.

A russet-coated cat stepped daintily over the sill and rubbed against his leg, huge emerald eyes glowing like green coals. Absently he bent and lifted it, holding it against his side, one hand fondling its fur. It flexed claws gently against his hand and then settled back, eyes closed, a husky purr beginning far down in its throat.

Forsythe didn't hear his secretary return. He stood in the same position until gradually he became aware of her. She was softly but urgently clearing her throat. He turned slowly, the beginning of a smile on his lips.

"Well?" he asked.

"That," she said, "is my line."

He regarded her fondly. She was almost his height, a thin, quick-moving woman with fine bones and a disciplined, almost austere face—a deceptively austere face.

"Give," she demanded.

Placing the cat on his chair, he leaned against the back of it. His smile broadened. "Elizabeth Calvert Pennell. Does the name ring any bell in that cross-index mind of yours?"

"Pennell doesn't. Hey, wait a minute, Robby; you said Calvert." She lifted her hand and began to click her thumbnail in an audible tattoo against her front teeth.

Forsythe sighed. "Sandy, can't you find some other way to stimulate your thinking processes without that infernal racket? I suggest biting your nails. It would be quieter, you know."

"You've suggested that before." Then her hand fell

away from her face. "She wouldn't by any chance be a relative of Sebastian Calvert?"

"You win again. His daughter, adopted in her infancy by Howard Pennell, her mother's brother." His glance was admiring. "I don't know how you do it."

Miss Sanderson flashed a grin at him. "It wasn't hard. The Calvert mess gets a large go-round by the yellow rags every time they're stuck for some nice gooey sensational stuff. You'd think it would have died years ago, but the weird circumstances around the whole deal and the group of people involved still make it a best-seller." Her face grew thoughtful and she slid into the chair that Elizabeth had occupied. "Sit down, Robby; I hate looking up at anyone."

Obediently, Forsythe circled the chair where the russet cat was sleeping and sat down next to his secretary. She looked at him closely, her eyes matching the pale blue sweater she wore.

"Just what did Sebastian Calvert's daughter want with you?"

"She wishes to reopen her father's case."

"For what purpose?"

"To establish his innocence."

Miss Sanderson gave a most inelegant, not austere snort. "Innocence! Blimey, that would be in the same league as attempting to prove that the Marquis de Sade was only a decent, fun-loving boy."

"Do you remember the case?"

"Well now, I was just a slip of a girl at the time . . ." Without looking directly at him, she seemed to sense his grin. "Anyway, I wasn't even close to thirty and doing my best to put up with your dad's idiosyncrasies the way I'm trying to put up with yours now. I remember the trial. It was a rushed affair, closed to the public, and in record time Calvert was judged guilty but insane and hustled off to someplace in the Midlands, Grey something . . ."

Forsythe reached for one of the papers on the desk and muttered, "Friar, Grey Friar."

"Right. A plush sort of place with maximum security. Funny thing was that at the time not too much public attention was given to the whole affair. Of course, the war was in its fifth year and I suppose that death had become commonplace. What was one murder more or less? Then again, the Calverts were very wealthy. There were still great fortunes. Sebastian was a prominent figure in the arts, so I guess that it was hushed up a certain amount."

Reaching in the pocket of her baggy tweed skirt, she pulled out a crumpled package of cigarettes. Forsythe lighted one for her.

"Knowing you, Sandy, I'm sure that you made it your business to learn all the lurid details. What was your opinion of the murder, and do you think there's any chance they might have gotten the wrong person? Calvert was never able to speak in his own defense, you know."

"My opinion . . ." She stopped and quoted solemnly, " 'Murder most foul, as in the best it is.' " Cocking one brow at her companion, she waited.

"My memory for the Bard isn't so bad either. Next sentence—'But this most foul, strange and unnatural.' "

"Very good, Robby. That pretty well sums it up. The world was younger then, less ready to accept the motive for the murder than it would be now. I can remember that even I was shocked at the time."

"You! I can't quite swallow that."

"You wouldn't have any idea of what a delicate shrinking maiden I was then. You were a mere broth of a boy staying with your mother's family in Scotland. Remember the lovely packages I sent you?"

"Black-market chocolates, among other things."

"It wasn't black-market, came directly from my own meager rations," she said indignantly.

"Seriously, what about Sebastian? Was it all that air-tight?"

"Couldn't have been more so. There were no actual eyewitnesses, but Calvert had the only motive and was caught literally red-handed." She blew a smoke ring and regarded it. "What did Miss Pennell say when you turned her down?"

"I didn't."

She almost dropped her cigarette. Turning sideways in her chair, she stared at him. "You can't mean you're taking this on! Raking up a bunch of mud and muck that should be over and forgotten."

"I'm taking it on, Sandy. As for the muck, as you said, it's raked regularly in the mags."

"This will be different." Her face was set and stern, all traces of levity had vanished. "You'll be working with the people closest to Calvert, the ones who have every right to try and forget. Besides, some of the mud that will be raked may be your own."

Forsythe's face remained adamant. She continued, an octave higher. "What right has Elizabeth Pennell to ask you to do this? She's no child, must be almost your own age. Why the sudden desire to clear a father she doesn't even know?"

His tone was level. "I rather think she's doing it for herself. Apparently she'd like to get married and doesn't dare expose the person she loves to the daughter of a man who is supposed to have killed horribly the one *he* loved. The point is, Sandy, I've agreed. Even you can't change my mind now. So," he reached over and plucked one of the slips of paper from the blotter, "here is a list of names. Write a nice polite note to each one and request an interview, mentioning Elizabeth's name and her relationship to Calvert. Be certain to stress that I'm doing this in a private capacity. Follow them up with phone calls wherever possible and ask for a date when I can speak with them. You can also make reservations for both of us at a hotel in London, someplace quiet."

Miss Sanderson glanced down the list of names. Her tone was as level as his. "Which one would you like to see first?"

"Might as well start with the solicitor who handled the defense."

"Firm of Meredith, Fuller, Meredith." She looked up. "Charles Meredith died last year. You'll have to consult with his son Peter. May run into some stickiness there. The old chap was a decent sort but his son . . ."

"I know. Went to school with him. We called him Porky. Suited him. But it can't be helped."

Forsythe rose, stretched, and moved to the chair behind the desk. Lifting the cat, he put it on the floor. It yawned, pink tongue curling out of the tiny red mouth, and stared up at him, its eyes wide and unblinking. After a moment it curled up on the carpet and resumed its nap.

"How did Miss Pennell get onto you in the first place?"

He handed her another sheet, this one heavy, cream-colored, embossed in gold. "Courtesy of Amelia St. Clair, reward for personal services."

Ruffling her short gray hair, Miss Sanderson gave another unladylike snort. "If you can call buying indiscreet letters from a slimy little blackmailer personal services, I guess she's right. Though it didn't save our Amelia in the long run, did it? Her husband ended up divorcing her anyway. I'll say one thing. She certainly can write love letters, didn't spare any details. They practically smoked."

Forsythe reached for a book and opened it. He glanced up from the pages and smiled at his secretary. "You do have lurid tastes, Sandy."

Shrugging one shoulder, she headed toward the door. "Perhaps. I will now go and make arrangements for Daniel to enter the lion's den."

Pausing, she stood with her back to him, her thumbnail beating its rhythm against her teeth. "Would you say your client was attractive?"

His face was puzzled. "Not in the ordinary sense of the word, but there's something about her—some quality. You might say she's a bewitching young lady."

The nail continued its drumming. "Did you know, Robby, in the seventeenth century there were covens of witches in England who actually offered human sacrifices?"

"Stop that racket, Sandy," he said impatiently. "Just what are you trying to say?"

She opened the door. Over her shoulder she threw one parting remark. "The majority of English witches bore the first name Elizabeth."

The door shut softly behind her.

CHAPTER 2

Forsythe tried to relax on the hard stone bench. Sandy had offered, almost insisted, on accompanying him for his interview with Meredith, but her offer had been refused.

Forsythe was glad he'd come alone. For the first time in six long years he'd walked the worn pavements of the Temple, gazed with nostalgic eyes at the smooth lawns, the Queen Anne and Georgian homes, felt the spray of the fountains against his face, and traced with lingering fingers the partially obliterated inscriptions on the sundials.

In a way it was a homecoming. The young law students passing him carrying beneath their arms sheaves of papers tied with traditional red ribbons reminded him of himself as he had been many years before, tall, serious, with a long narrow head and fine brown hair, a very young man in love with his mistress —the law.

There was a crowd in the Inner Temple today, tourists, employees from the offices on the Strand munching their lunches and enjoying the tranquillity of the ancient seat of law. He watched a young girl on the next bench. She was pretty in a pale way, dressed in bright, shoddy clothes. Solemnly she crumbled bread from her sandwich for a sparrow watching her alertly a few feet away. A strident voice frightened the bird and it winged away. Both the girl and Forsythe glanced toward the owner of the voice.

She was indubitably a tourist directing her smaller male companion's attention to a sundial. Much amused, Forsythe watched the tableau. The lady stationed herself in front of the sundial, nearly hiding it from view as the man readied his camera. He apparently wasn't handling the whole thing properly as he got a great deal of advice right up to the minute that he snapped the picture.

It had to be her husband, Forsythe decided; no one else could possibly maintain the forbearance he was showing. Forsythe wondered how the picture with the large woman in the foreground poised with a kittenish smile, one foot daintily turned out, and what appeared to be an outsize miniskirt straining across her bulging hips would look to the folks back home.

After several shots, they gave up the picture-taking and strolled toward Forsythe. The woman was busily reading aloud from a pamphlet.

"Says here, Henry, that even the Lord Mayor of London can be refused permission to enter here if he appears accompanied by his Sword and Mace Bearers." She stopped in front of Forsythe's bench, looked him over throughly, and demanded, "Is that true, young man?"

Courteously, Forsythe rose. She was even more intimidating at close quarters. "That is correct, madam. In fact, a Lord Mayor did violate that rule in the seventeenth century and was met by a group of students who demanded that he lower the City sword before entering the Hall. He refused and it ended in violence during which the Sword Bearer was injured. When Charles the Second was told about the riot, he asked the Lord Mayor to leave the Temple."

While his wife considered this morsel, Henry said timidly, "I understand a great deal of damage was done here during the last war."

"That's true, sir. Repairs have been made, of course, but many of the things destroyed can never be replaced. The Inner Temple Hall was gutted completely and the adjoining Library was destroyed, with a loss of forty thousand books."

The man nodded sympathetically but his wife decided to take a more militant attitude.

"Talking about books and buildings being destroyed! Think of the lads who lost their lives—"

"Madam," said Forsythe coldly, "think about the men, many of whom died trying to protect those books and buildings. Many things were destroyed but many others were saved. The people who offered their lives to protect them must have felt they had value or they wouldn't have done it."

Her mouth snapped open but the expression on Forsythe's face silenced her. With a toss of her head, she stalked off. Her small husband followed her. Behind her back he threw Forsythe a delighted grin and raised his hand in the V for victory sign.

Waving a hand at him, Forsythe sank back on the bench. He wondered when Meredith would condescend to see him. His clerk had informed Forsythe that his master was sorry to be late but he hoped to be free in an hour. Forsythe wondered whether it was only a way to humiliate him before the interview. Pushing up his sleeve, he glanced at his watch. The hour was nearly up.

He rose and began to retrace his steps. He was halfway there when he saw the clerk hurrying toward him.

"Mr. Meredith can see you now, sir, if you'll follow me."

"Is he waiting in his chambers?"

"No, sir; he has another trial starting in two hours so he's resting in an anteroom."

The clerk set off at a brisk pace. Forsythe followed his bent, black-clad figure across a stretch of lawn, through one paved court that led to another mulberry-colored one. The building they entered seemed eminently suited for the law. It was full of nooks and crannies, twisting passages, and unaired corridors. Forsythe breathed in deeply with a feeling of pleasure. The distinctive odor hadn't changed. It was impossible to define, consisting of hints of ancient parchment, ink, old leather, all overlaid with a mixture of dust and tobacco.

The clerk stopped so suddenly that Forsythe nearly walked up his heels. He opened a door softly, mentioned Forsythe's name, and then stood aside. Forsythe stepped into the room, aware that the door was closing just as softly behind him.

Meredith rose behind the deal table but didn't extend his hand. He looked warm and a trifle tired. His robe and wig were tossed over a chair and he wore a gray suit and a rumpled shirt.

"Well, Forsythe, it's been a while, hasn't it? Sit down, man, sit down."

He gestured with one hand and Forsythe sank into the chair opposite him. The table in front of Meredith was covered with law books and briefs, the remains of a lunch pushed to one side.

Forsythe studied his old schoolmate. Not much of the young Porky Meredith was left. The rolls of loose fat that had helped give him his nickname were missing. He was lean to the point of emaciation, but his nose was still the same, snoutlike with dark cavernous nostrils that faced the world squarely.

"I dug out the stuff your secretary said you wanted. How is Miss Sanderson anyway? Still as bright as ever, I'll wager. The full transcript of the trial is here and I threw in dad's notes on it. They may be of some help. Looked it over last night. I knew most of the details; bit of an obsession my dad had over it. Didn't want to take it on in the first place but had no choice. Our firm handled the legal affairs for the Calvert family for three generations, you know."

Meredith was speaking rapidly, disjointedly and Forsythe realized that he was nervous, unsure of what to say.

"Good of you to go to all this trouble, Meredith."

"I feel I should ask you one thing. What does Calvert's
daughter hope to gain by this investigation?" He didn't wait for
an answer. "I think she should keep clear of it. Her father had
a fair trial. Dad called in one of the best criminal barristers he
could get. Jacob Seburg, remember him? Died last year, a couple of months after dad's death. Supposed to be a boating
accident."

Forsythe broke in. "Supposed to be?"

"Common knowledge Seburg did himself in. Got involved with a girl young enough to be his granddaughter. She
was going to spill the beans to his wife and Seburg couldn't take
it. Can't for the life of me understand how a levelheaded man
can lose his head over a bit of fluff—" Meredith broke off,
avoided his companion's eyes as a flood of hot color inched up
his face.

Forsythe ignored his last remark and said cooly, "You
said your father was obsessed with this case. Do you think he
had any reservations about Calvert's guilt?"

"Not the slightest. Used the only defense possible, in-
sanity. No argument about that, Sebastian was crackers. The
whole affair sounds a trifle like one of those classical novels that
were written in the thirties. Old manse, chock-full of relatives
and guests, and then a murder. That's about the only similarity.
Nothing of a drawing room, tea, and good taste about this one.
Smelly affair. No, dad was upset because of Melissa Calvert and
her young niece. She wasn't much more than a child at the time
and dad did his best to keep her off the stand, but of course he
couldn't."

Neither man spoke for a moment. Meredith seemed to
be studying the dust motes floating in the band of sunlight that
spilled across the table. When he did speak his voice had
slowed. "Sorry to see you getting mixed up in this, Forsythe.

You don't *have* to do this sort of thing, do you? I mean I always understood you were all right financially, a fair income . . ."

He glanced up at Forsythe's set features. The tide of color that had receded came flooding back and he stuttered, "I'm deucedly sorry, old man, none of my ruddy business. Here," he rose and extended a cardboard folder, "keep these as long as you want."

"Thank you." Forsythe rose and accepted the folder, his movements a little stiff. He turned toward the door.

Meredith spoke behind him. "I wanted to tell you, Robert. Dad never did believe that scandal about you and the Telser woman. I think he'd have wanted you to know that."

Swinging back, Forsythe studied him. He asked softly, "And you, Peter, how do you feel?"

Meredith's eyes fell. "She was a most attractive woman. In fact, deucedly attractive. And you—well you were young and impressionable."

"Thanks for your faith." Forsythe bit off the words. Swinging open the door, he forced himself to close it gently. He stood quietly for a minute, fighting the tide of anger that was sweeping over him. Meredith's clerk scurried up, his hands full of papers. When he saw Forsythe he stopped, surprise on his face.

"You're finished, sir?"

"All finished." Forsythe brushed past him and strode down the corridor. He'd reached the entrance to the building when he heard his name called. Turning, he felt tense muscles relaxing. Hurrying across the stone floor was a familiar figure, a wide smile lighting his face, his hand outstretched.

Forsythe clasped the hand warmly. "Good to see you, Gene."

"I can't tell you how good it is to see you. Couldn't believe my eyes for a minute. So you have come back. I always knew you would."

"Sorry to disappoint you, but I'm only visiting."

"Visiting?" The man's face fell and he eyed the folder under Forsythe's arm.

"Picked it up from Porky Meredith, a personal matter."

"Well, when are you coming back? I mean for good."

Forsythe grinned. "What makes you think I have any choice?"

"Don't give me that stuff, Robert." He jerked his head at the corridor behind him. "The old school nicknames were always apt. Meredith is still a pig and you're still Foxy Forsythe. Someone did do some dirty work in the Telser case, but it damn well wasn't you."

Forsythe's smile broadened. "I'm glad I saw you, Gene. If you're ever in Sussex, look me up."

"How about lunch?"

"Already have a date with a gorgeous lady."

"Not Miss Sanderson, by any chance?" Forsythe nodded and his companion continued, "Will you be in London for a while?"

"A few days."

"Give me a ring and perhaps we can go out on a bash. Be like old times. Oh yes, give my love to Sandy."

"Righto."

With a flip of his hand, the other man headed down the corridor. Forsythe strolled through the mulberry court. A feeling of warmth and well-being filled him. The first hurdle had been taken. He strode through the Temple, crossed the Strand, and entered the restaurant where Miss Sanderson was waiting.

She was sitting at a corner table working methodically on a tall glass of amber fluid. This was a much different person from the Sussex Miss Sanderson. Her short gray hair was exquisitely coiffed and she wore a beautifully cut linen dress.

Forsythe slid into the seat opposite her and gestured at her glass. "I could use one of those myself."

At the same moment that she said, "Already taken care of," the waiter set a similar glass in front of Forsythe.

He took a long swallow of his whiskey and soda. "Most efficient. Have you ordered?"

"Lamb chops, a baked potato, and tossed salad. All right?"

"Fine." He glanced at her gleaming hair. "You made good use of your morning."

"That I did. First the hairdresser, and then some shopping." She fingered the sleeve of her dress complacently. "And how was your morning?"

"Better than I thought it would be. Porky managed to jab a few tender spots, but I think he was more embarrassed than I was. He gave me the impression he didn't quite know how to handle the situation, nothing in his books to cover it. Anyway, I have what we need. By the way, I ran into Eugene Emory. He wanted me to give you his love."

"Nice boy." Miss Sanderson glanced up as their orders arrived. They consumed the meal in silence. Over coffee she spoke again. "I managed to get onto Sir Hilary, at least to his man. He'll see you tomorrow morning. I also got in touch with Rosemary Horner." She stirred cream into her coffee. "I find I'm rather looking forward to seeing the terror of the courts again. Quite a man, Sir Hilary."

"One of the best minds in criminal law that this century produced. Good Lord, he must be close to a century himself."

"In his nineties and still clear as a bell mentally. He's in poor shape physically, had several strokes. His man, you must remember Hooper, asked me to make our interview as brief as possible. It seems strange to think of Sir Hilary as an invalid. He was so vital. What a life he had, three wives and countless mistresses."

Forsythe leered at his secretary. "Better watch yourself, Sandy; the old gentleman is or was a notorious rump pincher."

"Patter, and probably is rather than was," she said. "What about the balance of the day?"

"We will hie ourselves back to the hotel and spend the

afternoon and possibly the evening going over the transcript of the trial and Charles Meredith's notes with a fine-tooth comb."

"Exactly what will we be looking for?"

"Well, to acquaint ourselves with it. After that—God knows. Anything, a word, something that doesn't jibe."

She looked at the cardboard folder at his elbow. It was discolored with age and the ribbon tying it that had originally been red was now a faded pink. "Blimey, I feel like an archaeologist, about to dig among relics of the past."

Forsythe chuckled as he got to his feet and picked up the folder. "Come on, Sandy, let's have a go at opening the Pharaoh's tomb."

"With my luck," she said gloomily, "this is probably one that has an ancient curse attached to it."

CHAPTER 3

It all matched, the old house, the furnishings from another, gentler century, and the ancient man. The room was small, dark despite the early morning sunshine that peeked forlornly through the two tiny windows, and stuffy.

An electric heater glowed near Sir Hilary Putham's chair and a wool blanket was draped over his knees. Forsythe could feel his collar wilting and dampness gathering in the middle of his back. Even Miss Sanderson, clad in a light dress and holding a shorthand pad and pen at the ready, had a light film of perspiration dewing her forehead.

Sadly, Forsythe studied the old barrister. The big, virile figure that had dominated so many courtrooms was shrunken and wasted. All that remained were the bristling brows, snow-white now, that formed a bar over his deep-set eyes and the voice, still deep and resonant.

The famous voice boomed out now. "I won't have time for polite amenities. Hooper is quite capable of interrupting at any minute. He seems to do it as soon as things get interesting.

I think he's in a conspiracy with the damn doctor. Hooper always was something of a mother hen but now he's insufferable. However, I would like to mention that Abigail is as lovely as ever." He smiled at her. "And you, Robert, seem very fit. Country living must agree with you."

He braced his elbows on the arm of his chair, lifted his waxen fingers, and made a temple of them. "But you didn't come here to listen to this sort of thing. You're interested in the Calvert case. There's no use in going through it bit by bit; you've read the entire transcript, you say?"

Forsythe nodded. "Went through it yesterday, sir."

"Then what Miss Pennell wants and what you're looking for is a loophole, anything that might point to a miscarriage of justice. I'm afraid I can be of limited assistance there. Sebastian Calvert was the only person at the Hall who could wish Mersey dead. He had the opportunity and threatened the boy's life within hearing of all the witnesses. Above all, he was discovered by his publisher friend Deveraux with Mersey, or what was left of him, clutched in his arms. Horrible bit there. The local sergeant—good man he is too—managed to get pictures of Calvert and Mersey before they moved them. Ghastly things. I remember we had a long recess after the jury was shown the photographs. It must have been too soon after lunch and several of them went green."

Miss Sanderson shifted slightly. "You have a marvelous memory, Sir Hilary."

"Cheated a bit, my dear. Boned up on the case after I got your letter. But it's amazing how many of the details are clear. Of course, for me personally it was perhaps the most difficult case I ever had to prosecute. I knew Calvert slightly and I admired him. Tremendously talented chap, versatile. Wrote, painted, and sculpted. He wrote competently, was a good painter, but he excelled at sculpture."

Sir Hilary paused and gestured toward a decanter. "I'll have a small spot of brandy. Do you care to join me?"

Forsythe poured the drinks and handed each of his companions a glass. Sir Hilary sipped slowly, seemingly lost in his own thoughts. After a moment, without raising his eyes, he continued. "But it was more than Calvert that bothered me. His sister Melissa and I had once been very close. She's a great deal younger than I, but I've never considered age a detriment. There was a time I wanted to make her my wife. It was one-sided; Melissa couldn't take me seriously. In fact, she considered me a philanderer." Lifting his eyes, he slanted a smile at Miss Sanderson. "It may have been an apt term, but I've remained very fond of her. At the time of the trial I was forced to prosecute her only surviving brother. The older one, Allan, had been killed in the early years of the war. I think during the trial Melissa learned to hate me."

"Surely," this was Miss Sanderson, "she understood that you had to do it, that you had no choice."

"Melissa did understand that. What she hated me for was putting her niece, Rosemary Calvert, on the stand. Defense counsel did their best to keep her off, but her testimony was essential. I hated myself for doing it. Rosemary was only sixteen and at what I would suppose was the awkward age. A big, chunky child with that deplorable adolescent skin condition—"

"Acne?" Forsythe suggested.

"That's the one. The child was devoted to her uncle. A brilliant girl, sensitive and high-strung. She'd been in one mess in school after another. I must admit she stood up well under cross-examination. I had to tear every sentence from her bodily. It was a brutal job. I didn't blame Melissa."

He stopped, drew a deep breath, and lowered his voice. "Strange, as one gets older it's always the ones who got away that are remembered clearly. I can hardly recall what my first wife looked like and yet I remember Melissa Calvert well. She was the only woman I was ever attracted to who wasn't good-looking. An unattractive child and a plain woman. Yet I saw her a few years ago and she's one of those rare women who improve with age. She's quite stunning now. In the end, I suppose my taste was still operating."

"Your taste," said Miss Sanderson, "was always impeccable."

Sir Hilary placed one hand over hers for a moment. "Thank you, Abigail. But I digress. Old people are guilty of that frequently, I fear. To get back to the trial. You are both asking me the same question with your eyes. Was Sebastian Calvert guilty? Speaking only with logic, I'd have to say definitely. But two points have disturbed me for nearly a quarter of a century."

Forsythe had forgotten his discomfort from the heat. He leaned forward alertly. "What are these, sir?"

"The actual crime, its damn inconsistency. You know the details, of course?"

"By heart," Forsythe said. "David Mersey was killed from an overdose of morphine administered by hypodermic. At the time of the injection he was in bed, unconscious from the same barbiturate that the rest of the household had been fed. He was carried from his room to Sebastian's studio on the main floor, where his corpse was hacked to pieces with one of the swords from a display hanging on the wall, a scimitar. The following morning—"

"Right," said Sir Hilary. "And the hypodermic needle and the case that both the morphine and barbiturates were kept in were wiped clean of fingerprints. First the boy was drugged, then killed with morphine. He could just as easily have been carried down alive but unconscious and then killed with the scimitar. Now think of this, the first part of the crime executed in a quiet, painstaking way to avoid discovery of the murderer's identity. After all these precautions, Calvert lugs the body downstairs, across the hall, through the drawing room to his studio, and deposits it at the foot of the statue. There he carves the body up and throws down the scimitar covered with his fingerprints."

The old man shook his shaggy white head. "I have no idea why Meredith and Seburg didn't stress these facts at the trial. It was macabre, almost as though two murderers had been loose that night."

Forsythe smiled faintly. "If defense counsel had, what would the able prosecutor have flung back at them?"

Sir Hilary smiled also. "True. I would have insisted that after the first part of the crime Calvert's mind gave, and he was certainly mad, and the rest of it was the work of a maniac." His smile faded. "Yet, it has always bothered me." He put his glass on the table beside him and adjusted the plaid blanket. "However, it was the only explanation. The most damning thing in the whole trial was that the evidence that convicted Calvert came from the people who were valiantly trying to protect him —Melissa, his niece Rosemary, his secretary, his friend, and even his wife's cousin and companion—what was her name?"

Miss Sanderson's hand was flying over her notebook. "Atlin," she murmured, "Elinor Atlin."

"That's the one, a nice young woman, quiet, nothing like Vanessa."

"Vanessa Calvert," Forsythe said. "She was the only witness hostile to Sebastian, wasn't she? What was she like?"

Putham's expression changed. Suddenly he looked years younger. "Vanessa! A woman to weave dreams of, a memory to warm a man's heart when he's too old to warm it any other way. All the big, dramatic adjectives should be used to describe her because she was truly larger than life."

"Was she beautiful?" Miss Sanderson broke in.

"Beautiful, no. She was much too large to be beautiful or pretty or lovely. I said the big adjectives—*stupendous, marvelous, fantastic.* Vanessa must have been close to six feet tall and built to scale. Not one of your skimpy boy-women with no hips and breasts. Words can't describe Calvert's second wife. I think the closest I've ever seen was the other day in one of those sordid little books, an article rehashing the Calvert case, titled

'Why Did Davy Have to Die?' The title suited the writing—trashy stuff. But in one place, the author said that Vanessa had played Aphrodite to David Mersey's Adonis. I found that pleasing, suitable. Aphrodite, goddess of love. That *was* Vanessa, a goddess walking among mere mortals, one of the ancient goddesses terrible in her wrath—"

"I hate to interrupt," Miss Sanderson interjected dryly, "but from the transcript I'd say your goddess sounded more like a fishwife."

Sir Hilary regarded her quizzically. "You *are* very feminine, aren't you, Abigail? Cold words—and mere words on paper are cold—couldn't possibly give you any idea of Vanessa in the courtroom. She was aflame with vengeance, wouldn't believe for one moment that her husband was insane. She wanted Calvert dead and if we weren't willing to oblige, she was ready to draw and quarter him herself. I said terrible in her wrath. She was frightening, but at the same time I'll lay you odds there were few men present who wouldn't have sold their souls to possess her."

Miss Sanderson's jaw set stubbornly. "I still think—"

Forsythe stirred impatiently. "Before you start debating goddess versus fishwife, let me put a word in. I believe you said there were two points that disturbed you. You explained one. What was the other?"

Sir Hilary swung his eyes to Forsythe. "The first point was nebulous. The second is even more so. Have you seen the work that Calvert completed the day of Mersey's murder, his *Adonis?*"

Both his listeners shook their heads. "I thought not. Melissa wouldn't allow it to be shown for years. She was afraid of public reaction. I suppose she was right; the nature of the statue and the relationship between the sculptor and model would be enough to create a great deal of . . . shall I say, sordid speculation. However, about two years ago Melissa was finally persuaded to give permission for it to be shown at a small art gallery sponsored by private donations. Timed to be released at the same moment was another of those scurvy attacks on Calvert and his relatives, digging the same dirt up and rolling in it again. A close friend of mine was in the gallery when the public started to arrive. He said they flooded in, mobs of them, all walks of life. Apparently a lot of them had come to nudge each other in the ribs, the "ey, 'arry, fancy bloke, wasn't 'e' type of people. There was none of that. They saw the statue; they kept their filthy mouths closed; and they left rather stunned. You'd have to see it yourself to understand. I suggest you do." He handed Forsythe a slip of paper. "This is the address."

"But what—" Forsythe started to ask.

Sir Hilary lifted a hand. "I won't say any more. Just go, look at it, and arrive at your own conclusions. Now," he turned to Miss Sanderson, "would you indulge an old fellow and hold Hooper at bay for a few more minutes? He's due to come bursting in and there's something I'd like to say to Robert."

She was dismissed, however gently. Rising, she tugged her slim skirt down and closed her notebook. Smiling up at her, Sir Hilary maneuvered one arm behind her. Forsythe saw it move in a patting motion. He held his breath, waiting for Sandy's ever-ready temper to explode. She turned a bit pink but looked as though it was more in pleasure than in anger. Stooping, she brushed Putham's wrinkled cheek with her lips.

Putham's eyes followed her to the door. As it closed, he spoke to Forsythe without removing his gaze from the heavy oaken panel.

"You're a lucky man, Robert, and so was your father. There goes the most competent legal secretary in London. Just how are both of you making out in Sussex? How do you fill your time?"

"Reading, a certain amount of sports to keep in shape, and then there's a fair amount of social life. We've been working on the treatise on criminal law that father started. I have all his notes and it's shaping up fairly—"

"Great! A wonderful existence for two people like you."
The eyes under the bristling brows looked directly at Forsythe.
"A worthwhile project for you and Abigail."

Forsythe flushed. "Sandy came with me at her own
insistence. I tried to dissuade her—"

Sir Hilary cut him off again. "Loyal, my dear boy, as
many of your other friends have been loyal, waiting for you to
come to your senses. I'm very old, near the end of the road,
and I'm going to tell you a few truths other people have been
afraid to spill out. If you think I'm taking advantage of the
fact that I was a close friend of both your father and grandfa-
ther, you're absolutely right. I'll take any advantage I can
get."

"I know what you're going to say—"

"Then sit and listen without interrupting. At the time
of the Telser scandal, I was the person responsible for calling
the wolves off your trail. By exercising my influence—and I had
a fair amount—I was able to effect a gentleman's agreement.
You'd left your practice. Fine, if you stayed away from professional life, our fellow members of the bar agreed to leave you
alone. At the first indication that you intend to return to your
practice, they'll be on you. You'll have to clear yourself. I've
been patient. I've hoped that long before now you'd have tired
of your hopeless chivalry and decided to become a useful member of society."

The color had receded from Forsythe's fine features and
his face was pale. "At the risk of sounding ungrateful, sir, this
is my decision, my life."

"Your *life,* Robert? What kind of a life? You've buried
yourself in the country and you're engaged in an old man's life,
or I should say existence. You're trying to tell me to mind my
own business."

The booming voice faltered and he glanced down at his
hands folded on the plaid blanket. "You have a right to, my
boy, but can't you see that it's many people's business when a

man like you lies fallow? Give up this exile of yours, bring Abigail back to London, and pick up your practice. Clear yourself, I know you can."

"I'm going to use an old-fashioned word, Sir Hilary. My honor, I gave my word."

The elderly man threw up his hands. "Honor, misplaced chivalry. What about the fair maiden you rode forth to defend? I understand she remarried shortly after the trial and now has a young son. Her life goes on—"

Forsythe was on his feet. "I believe you presume, sir."

Sir Hilary sighed and laid his head against the chair back. He looked exhausted. "I believe I do, Robert. I was trying to tell you that knighthood is no longer in flower. The last of the knights-errant died many centuries ago. It's sad there isn't someplace in this modern world for them but, alas, there isn't. Abigail and yourself—that's a terrible loss. The people you could have helped . . . Believe me, Robert, you're acting more like Don Quixote than Sir Lancelot and you're forcing Abigail to be your Sancho Panza. There, I've said it all and I'm very weary."

The icy anger faded from Forsythe's face. He put his hand on Sir Hilary's shoulder and then turned toward the door. Sir Hilary spoke once more.

"If you uncover anything in the Calvert affair, will you let me know?"

His hand on the knob, Forsythe turned to face him. "I certainly will, sir; you'll be kept informed. Thank you."

Outside the door, Hooper was waiting. His wrinkled face was anxious.

"How is he, sir?"

"Very tired, Hooper, best you go in to him."

"I'll see Miss Sanderson and you out first."

"We'll find our way. How . . . how long do they give him?"

Anguish twisted in the faded eyes. "A few weeks, months. They can't really say."

Forsythe nodded. The smell of death had been in the small hot room. It had looked at him from the old man's eyes. As Hooper opened the study door, Forsythe walked slowly down the hall. In the foyer Miss Sanderson was bending over a strange object set in the middle of it. As he approached, she glanced up.

"I noticed this on our way in and couldn't believe my eyes. I still can't."

Forsythe stopped beside her. "It does shake you a little, doesn't it? Not very often you see a sundial in a house."

"Who put it here?"

"I have no idea. It's been here as long as I can remember."

"Why do you suppose Sir Hilary's kept it?"

Forsythe shrugged. "I've always thought it might be the inscription."

Bending over, she read the carved words. "The Wine of Life keeps oozing drop by drop. The Leaves of Life keep falling one by one." She raised her eyes. *"The Rubáiyát?"*

He nodded. "One of the lesser-known quotations. If there's one person who doesn't believe in missing one of those drops or leaves, it's our host."

Alertly, Miss Sanderson scanned his face. "He gave you a bad time." It was a statement, not a question.

"You know me too well, Sandy, or does the blood show?" He tried to grin. "There'll be time later to lick my wounds. Now I think we'd better get moving." He swung the heavy door open for her.

At the bottom of the steps, she looked over her shoulder at him. "Where away?"

"Where else but to see *Adonis* and try and figure out what Sir Hilary was driving at?" Under his breath he muttered, "Or to find one more windmill to tilt at."

Adonis stood in an alcove, a soft light shining on his marble form. Midnight blue silk fell gently behind him and a small metal plaque at his feet said simply: *Adonis*—Sebastian Calvert.

Forsythe and Miss Sanderson stood with their eyes riveted on Calvert's creation. The quintessence of male beauty lived in his face, his form. Somewhere Forsythe had read that this statue was often compared to Michelangelo's *David*. It shouldn't have been. This was no stripling, but a man in his prime, glorying in his strength and beauty. Marble was the material used by the sculptor, but under his hands marble had turned to living flesh, veins and muscular structure molding its surface. So lifelike was Adonis that Forsythe felt that at any moment the raised arm might lower and the figure would step off its pedestal.

Miss Sanderson was gazing at the face, the features serenely noble, a blend of intelligence and compassion. Her pale blue eyes were misted, and Forsythe had to strain to hear her words.

" 'O weep for Adonis—he is dead.' "

Her companion squeezed her arm in understanding and quoted from the same poem, " 'Peace, he is not dead, he doth not sleep—he hath wakened from the dream of life.' "

Digging in her handbag, Miss Sanderson found a crisp square of linen and touched it to her eyes. "I feel such a fool, Robby."

Still griping her arm he turned her away from the alcove. "Don't Sandy; if it wasn't considered unmanly, I'd shed a few tears myself."

"Sir Hilary was right."

"He was right. Whatever Sebastian Calvert was . . . well, he was no destroyer."

The attendant was waiting close to the street door. He was discreetly dressed in morning coat and striped trousers. Just as discreet was a silver salver on a background of black velvet close to his elbow. Forsythe placed a folded note on it.

The attendant carefully avoided looking at the donation.

Clearing his throat, he murmured, "What did you think, sir?" One hand delicately gestured toward the alcove.

Forsythe murmured back, "Not guilty." He raised his voice. "Definitely not guilty!"

Tugging at his sleeve, Miss Sanderson urged him through the door, onto the pavement. "The man thinks you mad. His mouth is falling open."

"Let him," said Forsythe grandly.

"This feeling we both have that we share with Sir Hilary, it's wonderful; but how do you think it will stand up in court?"

Forsythe eyed the vehicles moving by, the lumbering double-decked buses, the compact cars, an occasional chauffeur-driven limousine, with motorbikes darting erratic paths through them.

"The main thing is that now we are sure of our objective, which God knows we weren't before. Sir Hilary is a sly old devil; he's pointed the way. Now it's up to us to find proof. I'm going to put you into a cab and send you back to the hotel."

"But what about our lunch? I made arrangements at the hotel for a most scrumptious—"

"You eat it like a good girl. I'll pick up a sandwich on my way. This afternoon I want you to transcribe the notes you took this morning." He flagged a cab. "I'll go on and see Rosemary Horner." He noticed Miss Sanderson's wistful look. "If she'll consent, I'll tape her and you can hear the interview this evening."

The cab drew to the curb and Forsythe opened the door for his secretary.

"What if she refuses to be taped? I could come along and take notes."

"Uh, uh. I think she'll talk more freely if there's only one person listening. If she won't consent, I'll remember the pertinent points and dictate them to you later."

Reluctantly, his companion got into the cab. Sticking

her head out the window, she cautioned, "Take it easy with her husband. He's supposed to be something of a firebrand and he's a most important man in his profession."

Forsythe watched the cab drive off. He was lucky. In a few minutes he'd located another one and was headed in the opposite direction.

Leaning back against the cushions, he started to pack the bowl of his pipe.

" 'Weep not for Adonis,' " he mumbled.

He didn't realize he'd spoken aloud until the driver half turned and asked, "What's that, guvnor, say something to me?"

Forsythe's eyes traced his craggy profile, the lines of a greasy leather cap pulled low on his forehead.

"No," he said to the driver, "not really."

CHAPTER 4

John Horner's home didn't look like the house of an important man. It was a small villa, well-kept, cheerful but hardly pretentious.

Forsythe liked the looks of it and he liked the looks of the woman leading him into a rose-walled lounge. Rosemary Horner had made the transition from a chunky child with deplorable skin to an attractive matron with taffy hair hugging a finely shaped head. She was ten years older than her cousin Elizabeth, but looked younger. Turning, she smiled warmly at Forsythe.

"I was just thinking of having a gin and 'it.' Would you care for one?"

Placing his briefcase on the cretonne-covered divan, Forsythe smiled back. "That sounds fine, Mrs. Horner."

"Rosemary, please. I'll only be a moment."

Approvingly, Forsythe watched her leave the room. He was about to sink onto the divan when the photographs lined up on the chimneypiece caught his eye. Wandering over, he looked at them.

The one in the middle was a wedding picture. A radiant Rosemary smiled from the photo. Beside her, a short stocky man also smiled, although his was the forced grimace so many bridegrooms direct toward the camera in their nuptial pictures. The most striking of Horner's features was his jaw, hard and jutting and pugnacious.

Against the frame was propped a small snap of two boys dressed for cricket. The taller had a look of Rosemary about the eyes; the shorter was a smaller and younger replica of Horner.

"Our sons, Allan and John, Junior."

Forsythe swung around. He hadn't heard Rosemary enter the room. Her hands were empty.

"I thought we might sit in the garden. It's such a beautiful afternoon and the house seems stuffy."

Nodding, Forsythe picked up his briefcase. Patting it, he asked her, "Do you mind if I use a tape recorder? It's much more accurate than notes or relying on memory."

"Of course not, if it will help."

It was pleasant in the garden. Under a large flowering tree, their drinks waited on a white iron table. Wicker chairs with bright cushions were arranged around it. Gesturing at one chair, Rosemary sank into another.

"I can't tell you how glad I was to get your letter. The mere thought that someone cared enough to look into my uncle's case was heartening. My cousin must be a wonderful person."

Forsythe looked up from the machine he was adjusting. "Have you not seen her?"

She shook her blonde head. "Of course, Elizabeth may have tried to contact Aunt Melissa. My aunt's in Scotland. She took our boys with her for a short trip. So Elizabeth is probably waiting for her return."

Remembering the look on Elizabeth's face as she'd spoken of her father raising Rosemary, Forsythe mentally shook his own head.

"Now," he said, settling back in the chair and lifting his glass, "I know that this will be difficult for you, but I'd like to have you tell me what you remember. Any detail, no matter how insignificant, may help. I'll ask you one question. Do you believe your uncle guilty?"

"No." The wide-set eyes, more gray than blue, met his. "I never have and I never shall."

"The evidence against him was overwhelming."

"I realize that. You'd have to have known Sebastian as I did to be convinced that he was incapable, not of violence, but of that type of murder. He was temperamental at times, but basically he was gentle, understanding. My father was Allan, his older brother. Father divorced my mother when I was seven. She remarried in record time and my father gained custody of me. He was a professional soldier, stationed in India at the time. Father found he was not able to raise a child by himself, so he sent me back to England, to Aunt Melissa and Sebastian. My aunt was competent; she was the one who chose my schools and looked after my needs, but it was Sebastian who gave me all the attention I ever got."

Breaking off, she gazed down into her glass, swirling it so the pink bitters lanced through the icy silver of the gin. "My childhood was most unsettled and I didn't help any. I was in scrapes at school continually. It was always Sebastian who came to the rescue and bailed me out."

Forsythe interrupted. "Could you tell me something of your uncle's background?"

"Well, as you may know, he gained an international reputation in the art field as a very young man. Sebastian married fairly young, when he was twenty-four. His first wife, Mary Ellen Pennell, was one of those milk-and-water females. You know the type—loved being the wife of a famous artist and playing lady of the manor. I never had the impression she liked anything else that went with it. She struck me as the kind who would consider the nuptial couch an instrument of torture."

Forsythe felt his lips twitching. "You must have been a most precocious child, Rosemary."

She gave him a gamin grin. "That I was, a holy terror. Anyway, when I was nine Mary Ellen became pregnant and her whole world went topsy-turvy. She treated poor Sebastian as though he alone was responsible for it and lay around as though she was about to die at any minute. The damndest part of the whole business was that she did die when Elizabeth was born. My uncle was desolate, more with guilt than grief, I would imagine. He wanted no part of the baby and as Mary Ellen's brother and his wife were childless, it worked out well.

"Sebastian seemed much calmer after they left for America. He went to work with a vengeance and did several good things in that period. All was fairly serene until war broke out. Sebastian couldn't get into the forces. His left leg had been injured when he was a boy and he walked with a slight limp. Then in forty-one, he met and married Vanessa. It was a whirl-wind courtship and I didn't meet her at that time.

"Vanessa and Sebastian went to Ireland for their honey-moon and stayed there for nearly a year. For that year I was inconsolable. I guess that Sebastian was a symbol, the only security I'd ever known, and he had left my life. He wrote me a couple of letters during the first month and then he didn't write anymore. I reacted like a pint-sized demon and Melissa was just about at the end of her tether with me.

"Then my aunt wrote that Sebastian had returned to the Hall alone. I went home even though it was the middle of the term, took French leave and just walked out. Sebastian looked like death. He had no interest in me or anyone else. My aunt forced me to go back to school, but promised she would let me know how he was. Sebastian improved physically, but he'd lost all desire to work. His work was important to my aunt. I imagine even then that Aunt Melissa knew that Sebastian would never have a son to carry on the name and the name was an obsession with her."

Forsythe leaned forward. "Your aunt wished Sebastian's fame to compensate for the end of the family line?"

"Exactly. A type of immortality you could call it. I believe she did everything in her power to rouse him from his —what would you call it?—depression, resignation. In September of forty-three, Sebastian went to London to visit Richard Deveraux and he returned with David."

"Adonis," said Forsythe.

The bright head nodded. "Adonis. From then on Sebastian worked like a madman—" she stopped and the clear eyes clouded. "The terms we use."

"We all do," Forsythe said gently.

"We shouldn't. But to continue. Sebastian came back to life. Melissa was delighted. She was pushing herself too hard trying to run that huge house with practically no help and was involved in war work up to her ears. Next to Sebastian's work, she was obsessed with patriotism. She literally drove the villagers into every type of civil defense you could think of. Of the three Calverts, Aunt Melissa had the strongest will. Neither my father nor Sebastian had her willpower."

Rosemary paused. "Is all this what you want, Robert?"

He choose his words carefully. "It's necessary. The data from the trial isn't enough. I have to sift through the lives of these people. Somewhere in the strands there may be a clue. Please continue."

He'd spoken sincerely. From cardboard cutouts the people involved in the murder were beginning to take shape, to assume flesh and blood.

He prompted. "In May of forty-four you returned home."

"In disgrace, or I should say that without Sebastian it would have been disgrace. As I mentioned, my school record was vile; I had a frightful temper. This was my last and worst mess.

"We had this games mistress, one of those great muscular women with an incipient mustache. I always suspected she had too many male hormones and her actions bore this theory out. Always with her hands on one of the girls, you know.

"Early in the term I'd shown her it was hands off with me and from there on she had it 'in for me' as we used to say. The morning it happened she asked me a question and I answered. I don't really remember what it was all about. The upshot was that she called me a liar and struck me in front of the whole class.

"The next thing I remember two of the teachers were pulling me off her. She was sprawled on the ground, quite red in the face, holding her throat. I'd gone berserk and knocked her down. Then I'd grabbed her head and banged it on the ground.

"They hauled me away and locked me in my room. Then they phoned my uncle and told him I'd become homicidal. Sebastian arrived like a knight on a white charger." Forsythe winced at the words, but Rosemary didn't notice. "In record time he cleared the whole thing up, forced the teacher to confess there had been provocation, and extracted an apology from the headmistress. She even wanted me to stay on in school, but Sebastian grandly announced that his niece would never return to a school that employed teachers of poor caliber."

Rosemary had been speaking rapidly; now she paused to catch her breath. She continued more slowly. "We went home. Aunt Melissa reluctantly agreed that I was to stay until the fall term and the next few months were a Utopian time in my life. There were five of us at the Hall—Sebastian, Aunt Melissa, David, and, of course," she smiled, "John."

"You met your husband at Calvert Hall?"

"I met a young poet whom Sebastian had taken under his wing. John had been invalided out of the army and was acting as his secretary. I don't think John knew I existed, and as far as I was concerned—well, he was a weird young man who reminded me of a bantam rooster running around with his hands full of papers. We met later in London, years after the trial. I was in art school . . . but we don't have to go into that, do we?"

"Tell me a little about it, Rosemary."

"It was the turning point of my life. I was twenty-five and had never considered marriage, children. The murder, the trial, all those people staring at Sebastian's niece. Can you understand what I'm trying to say?"

Across Forsythe's mind flashed another woman's face, a dark face with brilliant black eyes. "A normal life," those were Elizabeth's words.

Rosemary read the understanding in his face. "John changed all that. We married; Allan and Johnny were born; and yet . . . I don't think I'll ever really lose the apprehension. I hold my breath when either of the boys get annoyed, even boyish anger. It's foolish but to me it's real." She straightened in her chair. "But I've learned to live with it."

Forsythe wondered if she had. Her composure was not as perfect as it had been. He could see the strain on her face.

"If you'd prefer, Rosemary, we can finish this later . . ."

"No, let's go on. Back to forty-four. Strange the scattered impressions I get looking back at that summer. I can see David, the sun gilding his body as he dived into the lake; Sebastian at the end of the day coming out of his studio with a smile on his face—I waited for him every night. I remember the meals, the dreadful meals. Aunt Melissa was a stickler for using only our rations. Not that I'm advocating the black market, but she could have gotten extra eggs and milk from the tenant farmers. Not Aunt Melissa; you would have thought an egg would sabotage the entire war effort. I was always hungry. I'm making my aunt something of a monster, aren't I? She wasn't, just—"

Rosemary broke off abruptly and laughed. "I'm becoming disjointed. Could you help me back on the track?"

"Vanessa and Elinor Atlin arrived in August. Fill in the months between."

"The months between." She drew a deep breath. "As I said, it was a wonderful time. Sebastian worked hard but he was so happy. Aunt Melissa was wrapped up in her auxiliaries but she found enough time to involve me as much as she could. I helped in the local hospital as an aide. Much of my spare time was spent with David Mersey. He enjoyed the same things I did. Between us we cleaned up the tennis court; it hadn't been used in years. And we swam and hiked, went down to Meads Green quite often. That sort of thing." She looked at Forsythe. "Those were the months before Vanessa arrived."

"You say you spent a great deal of time with Mersey. Did you have any idea about your uncle and him?"

"You mean," Rosemary said quietly, "did I know they were lovers? You said I must have been precocious. I was. Years in a girl's public school only made me more so. I knew about that sort of thing, all the grubby names. Yes, I was aware they were homosexuals."

"It didn't bother you?"

"Bother me? No. You must realize, Robert, I idealized Sebastian. I never really reasoned it out. I suppose I felt that whatever was good for him had to be right. David definitely was. They were different from my notions of . . . well, fags. David was incredibly handsome and very masculine, and there was nothing overt. Whatever happened privately between them had no part in our day-to-day life. If you knew Aunt Melissa you'd be certain that if it had, she never would have allowed me to return."

"And Melissa, did she know?"

"She must have, but she never let on."

"Let's get back to Mersey. What was he like?"

"Handsome, but I've said that. Very physical. He had

gym equipment in the basement and worked out regularly. Mentally, rather slow as so many of that type are. He'd been brought up in Limehouse. I think he'd been a dockworker, and you'd expect him to be crude. He wasn't. Aunt Melissa said he was much like a chameleon. He aped superbly—dress, manners —he even spoke fairly well. You could see him watching us, trying to do things the same way as we did, speak the same way. I'm not being very helpful, am I?" She rose. "I'd forgotten. I have something that might help. Excuse me."

Forsythe watched her walk up the flagstone path to the house. She moved well, with a balanced grace. Flicking off the recorder, he rose and paced back and forth, a slight frown pulling his brows together. Rosemary was trying hard, too hard, and it was taking its toll.

She was gone only a short time. When she returned, she opened a large sketchbook and gestured to Forsythe.

"These are the sketches I made that spring and summer. Not terribly professional, but I feel I've caught many of them."

Forsythe bent over the table and examined them with interest. The first one was labeled "Sebastian." Elizabeth was very much her father's daughter. Sebastian had the same dark eyes, the high-bridged nose. There was a hint of her arrogance, but her father lacked the strength around the mouth and chin that his daughter had.

Forsythe turned the page. A dark-eyed woman gazed from it, the same features, her hair neatly waved back from her brow. This time the resemblance to Elizabeth was startling. There was no name on this one.

"Aunt Melissa," Rosemary murmured.

The next face he recognized. He was younger but the chin was the same. The mouth was more vulnerable. Forsythe spoke before Rosemary could.

"Your husband."

"Yes, and this is David."

Rosemary had been modest. This one was professional.

Without asking, Forsythe knew that the thick wavy hair was blond, the large, long-lashed eyes blue. This was the face of the statue, but there was some difference. Rosemary was watching him.

"It's the expression," she said.

"Are you a mind reader as well as an artist?"

"Not much of either, I'm afraid. You mentioned when you arrived that you'd just been to see Sebastian's *Adonis*. I have no doubt my uncle did see in David's face the qualities he gave *Adonis*. But David was not *Adonis*. He was merely a very beautiful male animal with an expression of good nature, nothing else."

Forsythe started to turn the page. Rosemary put her hand on it. "Not yet, please. We'll get to the last two."

They returned to their chairs and Forsythe started the tape.

She looked questioningly at him. He prompted her again.

"August and Vanessa."

She gave him a lopsided grin. "Or should we say, enter the serpent into the garden of Eden? Paradise doesn't last forever. Ours didn't. On the twelfth of August, without any warning, Vanessa arrived. She came like a bolt from the blue with mounds of luggage and Elinor Atlin.

"I wasn't at the house when they got there. David and I were swimming in the lake. Melissa was still treating me like a small child, and I wasn't allowed to go down alone. When we got back to the Hall, we entered through the side door, still wearing our swimsuits. We heard voices from the drawing room. I wandered in and there Vanessa sat, her shoes kicked off, smoking a cigarette and looking amused. Aunt Melissa looked like death. But there was nothing she could do. Vanessa was Sebastian's wife and had as much right there as any of us."

Rosemary paused, felt in the pocket of her skirt, and asked her companion, "Do you have a cigarette?"

He offered her his case and a light. Sitting back, she inhaled deeply. Then she continued. "I'm trying to remember who was there. Sebastian had already seen Vanessa; I heard that later. Oh yes, Elinor was standing beside Vanessa's chair, very awkward and ill at ease. John was watching Vanessa. He couldn't see anyone else from the moment she arrived. When I came in, Aunt Melissa started to introduce me but Vanessa wasn't paying any attention. She was staring past me. I looked around and David was behind me, still in his bathing trunks. And—"She broke off and the gamin grin touched her lips again. "David in trunks was something to see. Melissa introduced David to the two women. Then she spoke sharply to David and me, told us to get upstairs and get some dry clothes on.

"Vanessa got up and stretched, slowly, you know. She said she might as well get settled. It ended up with her leading the way and David, Elinor, and me carrying all her luggage. Vanessa allowed me to stay while they unpacked; at that point I don't think she could have driven me out.

"Her clothes! Mounds of beautiful, yummy things. Real silk stockings, piles of lingerie. Everything was color-coordinated, shoes and hats for each suit and dress. It nearly took my breath away. You must remember, I was used to wartime England, everyone slightly shabby and drab. Where Vanessa got this wealth of goodies from, I still don't know.

"Vanessa pumped me about David—who he was and why he was there, why he wasn't in the services. I couldn't answer that. When she had all I knew, she gave me a pair of stockings and a tiny bottle of scent and got rid of me. Aunt Melissa, of course, made me give them back later."

Forsythe broke in. "What was your impression of Vanessa? Do you have a sketch of her?" His hand moved toward the book.

"No. I did ever so many but tore them all up. I couldn't get her. Her features came out fine but not . . . well, her. As for Vanessa, I don't know how anyone could describe her. After what she did to my uncle I suppose I should have hated her. But just walking into the room and seeing her, dressed all in white, a great mass of hair resting on her shoulders, one was impressed. She wore it in the style so popular in the forties. A high pompadour and a roll on the shoulders. Her hair was very long when it was down, nearly to her waist, flaming hair, a true red-gold. I could describe her appearance but it wouldn't help."

"You didn't hate her."

Rosemary spread her hands expressively. "How could I? It would be much like trying to hate a natural force, a typhoon, a hurricane. You might hate what they *did,* the havoc they wreaked, but you couldn't hate them."

"And she did start to wreak havoc."

"It started the minute she arrived. The little group that had been so placid was gone and was replaced by . . . Well, John was mad for Vanessa. He followed her around and scribbled poems about her. Aunt Melissa was all nerves; she acted terrified of what Vanessa would do to Sebastian. I couldn't do anything right. Clumsy, within the first week I'd sat on and smashed my aunt's glasses—and she was lost without them; my kitten and I managed to ruin a batch of knitting she was working on; and, oh yes, I broke a kitchen window. I suppose Aunt Melissa had good reason to be snappish with me and she was. In the meantime, Vanessa was in pursuit of David, had her hands on him at every opportunity."

"How did Mersey react to that?"

"He seemed dreadfully embarrassed and avoided her as much as possible. David, Elinor, and I spent a great deal of time together. Elinor was as athletic as we were. We went swimming, played tennis, hiked into Meads Green. Anything to keep away from Vanessa."

"What about Elinor?"

Rosemary turned a page in the book. "Here she is, or was then. A big woman like her cousin. Her parents were missionaries and she certainly looked the part. She wore steel-rimmed glasses, flat shoes, dowdy clothes, and had her gingery hair pulled straight back in a bun. She was Vanessa's age, about twenty-eight. Elinor was quiet, devoted to Vanessa but appalled by her at the same time. A nice woman."

Turning the page, Rosemary said, "And here is the last one, Richard Deveraux, Sebastian's good friend."

Richard Deveraux looked from the page with humorously sardonic eyes. He had a good face, firm mouth and chin, aquiline nose. Thick hair was brushed back from a perfect widow's peak.

"A fine-looking man."

"And a fine man, Robert. Aunt Melissa sent out an SOS for him during the first week of Vanessa's stay. Richard arrived the following Sunday. Vanessa was away that weekend visiting friends a few miles away. She returned the next morning—Monday."

"About Sebastian, how did he react to Vanessa's attentions to Mersey?"

Rosemary pushed a strand of hair from her forehead. "Of all of us Sebastian seemed the least affected. Of course, he was working on his *Adonis* and he carefully avoided his estranged wife. He even took most of his meals in his study or studio. Perhaps he didn't realize the extent of Vanessa's infatuation, or maybe he felt too sure of David. Whatever the reason, Sebastian was the calm in the middle of the hurricane."

Taking a small notebook from his pocket, Forsythe consulted it. Rosemary watched him silently.

"Wednesday night the hurricane began to gain force, didn't it?"

"For Aunt Melissa and me, yes. That would be on record in my testimony at the trial, wouldn't it?"

"The outline is. Could you fill it in?"

"I was starved Wednesday night. When we went to bed —my aunt and I were sharing the same bedroom—all I could think of was the remains of a cold chicken in the icebox. I drifted off to sleep but awakened around three, famished. Aunt Melissa seemed sound asleep so I crept out of bed and headed down to the kitchen. She must have had a mental alarm. No sooner was my hand in the icebox when I heard her voice behind me. She said something like, 'Get to bed!' and stalked into the hall ahead of me.

"Both of us were used to the layout of the house and she didn't turn on the lights. We padded up the stairs; I was in bare feet and she wore soft slippers. We were near the top when I heard a man's voice and a woman laughed, a deep, throaty laugh. There was a dim light in the upper hall and I had a glimpse of Vanessa leaving David's room. Then I was pushed back against the wall by my aunt. I stood there holding my breath—"

"Let me get this straight, Rosemary. Mersey's room was the first one, closest to the stairs."

"That's right. When Aunt Melissa figured the coast was clear, we returned to our room. I crawled into bed and lay there shaking. My aunt paced up and down for a moment, not really wringing her hands, but very close to it. Then she told me to go to sleep. She left the room. When she came back, I pretended I was asleep and I heard her crying. That really shattered me. My aunt is not the sobbing type of woman."

"And the next day David was still pretending to avoid Vanessa?"

"He acted just the same. I remember looking at him and wondering what kind of an actor he was. Yet there was Vanessa coming out of his room. I can still see her, her long hair falling down her back, one of her negligees, a pale blue one, flowing around her. Both Aunt Melissa and I knew that she had won."

"Did either of you let on to Sebastian?"

"I felt he should be told, but Aunt Melissa ordered me not to mention it. The following night, Thursday, Richard—"

"Yes, I know what Richard saw and did."

Rosemary was pale and drawn now. Lines showed

around her eyes and mouth that Forsythe hadn't noticed before. He made a move to turn off the recorder. She stopped him, her fingers cold against his hand.

"Please, I'd like to finish."

"Wouldn't it be easier at another time? You look exhausted."

"It will never be any easier. Friday, the twenty-fifth of August, was the last day. It marked the end of one life, the beginning of another.

"I was helping Aunt Melissa prepare breakfast. Our old cook was not well and the only other help we had, a girl from the village, wasn't there. The morning was so beautiful that my aunt decided to serve breakfast on the terrace. It runs right along the west side of the Hall. Everyone but Sebastian and Vanessa was at the table. I didn't think anything of their absence. Vanessa usually slept late and Sebastian's meal hours were irregular."

"Your aunt didn't tell you that Sebastian knew about Mersey and Vanessa?"

"She didn't say a word. The first thing I knew about it was when we heard voices from the sunken garden, just below the terrace. They became louder and louder until we could hear every word. It was Sebastian and Vanessa. They were quarrelling violently about David.

"Sebastian was bringing up dreadful things that had happened during their marriage and Vanessa was throwing insults back at him. I was sent upstairs just after they got started, but I went into Richard's room; it was right over the terrace. From there I could not only hear them, I could see them. Sebastian was flushed and furious and Vanessa looked as though she was enjoying herself. She seemed to thrive on violence."

Forsythe checked his notes again. "This was when Sebastian made his threat."

"Vanessa was taunting him. She said, 'What can you do

to stop me? I may even leave and take David with me.' My uncle just roared, 'I'll stop you. You'll never have a chance to do to that boy what you did to me!' She laughed. I can still see her laughing, her head thrown back, the sunlight on her face. She said something about David preferring a real woman to a fag like Sebastian. I thought for a moment he was going to strike her. He raised his arm, then he lowered it slowly and said, 'I'll see him dead first.' "

"The most damning piece of evidence at his trial."

"Everyone heard that. The next part, the reason I was forced to testify at the trial, came later. I remained upstairs, just lying across the window seat in Richard's room. In some ways I was a woman, in some still a child. The child came out when I looked out of the window and saw David heading for the lake in his swimming trunks. Badly as I felt, I went to my room, changed into my bathing suit, and followed him—very cautiously and quietly. I didn't want Aunt Melissa to catch me. I knew she had meant me to stay in our room."

"Elinor Atlin followed Mersey too."

"She was there first. I'd just about reached the lake when the loose lace on my sneaker tripped me. I knelt down to tie it. I wasn't trying to eavesdrop. "At the time I didn't know Sebastian had already taken David into his study for a talk. When I approached the lake, I found that Elinor had followed David and they were talking. I heard a few words and then I listened."

"Can you remember the exact words?"

"I should be able to; I had to go over and over it at the trial. 'Then you've made your choice?' Elinor asked David. He said, 'I have.' She asked him, 'Did you tell Sebastian?' David said, 'I did. I'm sick of being pulled two ways. I'm my own man and I'll do as I damn well please.' Then Elinor said something about ruining his life and he didn't say anything for a minute. I couldn't catch the next few words, but then he mentioned Vanessa's name. Elinor made a sound like a short laugh and said, 'Don't worry about me. I've been deserted before by Vanessa—when she married Sebastian.' "

"Did you understand what Elinor was alluding to?"

"Not at that time. Later I learned that the only time the cousins had been parted was the year of Vanessa's marriage to Sebastian, when they remained in Ireland. But to get back to the lake. The next thing Elinor said was 'You don't seem to realize what this will do to your life.' David muttered that it was his own affair, and Elinor started down the path toward me. She called back, 'You may regret it.' I was busy getting out of the way. I needn't have worried. Elinor went right past and didn't see me."

"Adonis," said Forsythe, "had chosen Aphrodite."

Rosemary said somberly, "He'd also chosen death. I went back to the house. I was so worked up I found Aunt Melissa and blurted the whole thing out. She took me up and put me to bed. I was nearly hysterical. My aunt was very gentle and kind. I didn't see any of them until evening. Aunt Melissa brought my dinner up on a tray. She was trying to make me feel better and had put a glass of cream soda on it. I drank that, but I couldn't eat a bite of food. After they'd dined she came up and got me. Sebastian wanted—"

Rosemary's voice had been rising. Concerned, Forsythe looked up from his notebook. Tears glazed her eyes and were trickling down her ashen face. She was groping blindly in her pocket. He rose and handed her his own handkerchief.

She sobbed. "I thought I was going to be such a brick, get through the whole thing." Groping for the handkerchief, she dabbed at her eyes. "I saw them. Sebastian clutching that awful thing in his arms. David had been disemboweled. His neck was nearly severed. Sebastian's clothes, his hands were covered with—"

"Don't. Let it go." Gently, Forsythe pulled her to her feet, put one arm around her shaking shoulders. "I've been a ruddy ass. I should have had more sense."

A voice spoke behind Forsythe, grinding the words out.

"You're damn right you should! What do you think you're doing to my wife?"

Without releasing Rosemary, Forsythe glanced around. John Horner was watching them, his eyes far from friendly.

Rosemary wiped her face and pulled away from Forsythe's arm. "Don't be a ninny, John. Robert's not the ass; I am. I'm acting like a neurotic."

Her husband's expression relaxed a trifle. He slid an arm around her waist. "Neurotic or not, my dear, you're all through for today. I'm going to take you to the house and you're going to rest for a bit."

She didn't protest. She only looked searchingly at her husband and asked, "Will you talk to Robert?"

"I'll talk to him." He led her away. Over his shoulder he flung at Forsythe, "Wait for me in the shed. The door isn't locked."

Gathering up his recorder and briefcase, Forsythe looked in the direction Horner had pointed. Almost hidden by an arbor was a good-sized shed. It looked like a tool or potting shed. One end of it had been torn out and a large pane of glass installed. Inside he found that the center of the splintery floor had been covered with a piece of garish linoleum and someone had tacked green wallboard over the studs. Other than that it was still very rough. A discarded kitchen table sat squarely in the middle of the floor with two straight chairs near it. Arranged on the table was a typewriter, a bottle of scotch, and two glasses. The floor was littered with untidy piles of books, magazines, and paper.

He was setting up his tape recorder beside the typewriter when Horner returned and stood straddle-legged beside the door.

"You might just as well pack that stuff up." Horner gestured toward the recorder. "I've spent most of the day trying to head you off. They said at your hotel that you were expected back for lunch. Your secretary arrived alone, so I knew you'd reach my wife before I could stop you. Since then I've been walking around trying to cool off." He didn't look like he had succeeded. "I'm going to give you some advice. For your own good I'd suggest you take it."

Forsythe kept his voice friendly. "If it's sound, I certainly will try."

"It's sound. Drop it. Drop the whole business and clear off. Don't ever approach my wife again and leave her aunt alone."

"Why?"

"I checked you out when we got your letter. Found out you had gotten involved in an unsavory affair a few years back. No discredited shyster is going to put my family through this hell. Raising hopes in a couple of poor women who have had all they can take of this, for some shoddy little scheme of your own."

"Hardly my own, Horner. I was retained by your wife's cousin."

"I don't give one damn for some cousin my wife's never even seen. Now get your junk and get out."

"How do you think your wife will feel when she finds you wouldn't even try to clear her uncle?"

"Blackmail now, by God! You'd better leave before I throw you out."

Forsythe could feel his own temper snapping. "Would you like to try? I'll leave in a minute, but before I go I'm going to tell *you* something. I've had quite a day and I'm in the mood. In the first place I didn't want to get involved in this. But Elizabeth Pennell deserves this much and, although I thought it hopeless, I agreed to try. Do you think I enjoyed your wife reliving the whole damn nightmare again? You must know what is at the back of her mind. Looking at her two boys, wondering—"

"That's bloody nonsense. My boys are not their great uncle. The chances of them being like him are so remote it's ridiculous."

"I agree with you, but I don't think Rosemary does. If there's any chance of giving her peace, wouldn't it be worth it?"

Horner seemed to have simmered down a bit. He thought for a minute. "You said yourself it's hopeless."

"I thought that at the beginning. This morning I took the advice of a man who knows what he's talking about and went to see the *Adonis.*"

Horner looked puzzled. Slowly he closed the door and walked over to the table. "And?"

"You're a creative person yourself. Any writer with your following has to be. Can you really believe that the man who expressed the love that Calvert did in that chunk of marble could kill the boy who inspired it in the *way* he did? He would be as incapable of an act like that as of smashing the marble *Adonis* to bits."

"Calvert was tried and convicted. All the evidence, the motive—"

Forsythe cut him off curtly. "He was tried as much for his sexual behavior as for his supposed crime. Sebastian Calvert's mind was gone. He was a pervert in the eyes of the world. Just how thoroughly did they sift to try and find motives for the rest of you?"

"Motives?" Horner ran his hand through his shock of graying hair. "Who else would have wanted to see the boy dead?"

"That," said Forsythe shortly, "is what this discredited shyster is trying to find out."

All heat had left the other man's face. Pulling out a chair, he slumped on it, waving Forsythe to the other.

"Sit down. You have an apology coming. I fire off too fast, always have, and you're entirely different than I pictured you. Very well, I'll cooperate. Turn your tape on but," he shot a piercing look at Forsythe, "remember I'm doing this not because of your threat about Rosemary but because I owe it to her and to Sebastian Calvert."

His brow furrowed and he looked past Forsythe. "I owe a lot to Calvert. In the fall of forty-three, I was invalided out of the army. I'd been in the North African campaign and got badly shot up. When I wrote Calvert I was a mess. Most of my money was gone; I had to help my parents and I was down to my last few pounds. I still wasn't recovered physically and my nerves were in worse shape than my body. I couldn't hold an ordinary job.

"I'd met Calvert some time before and he'd expressed interest in my work. I wasn't a novelist then; I was working in poetry." He broke off and grinned, his face suddenly charming.

"It's a good thing my prose is better than my verse. Calvert saw something in me even then. He sent me a ticket to Meads Green, and I went to live at the Hall. He made a job for me that wasn't too demanding so I wouldn't feel a charity case."

"David Mersey was already there when you entered the picture."

"Yes, Mersey and Calvert were right in the middle of a hot little love affair. As a real man's man straight out of the army I was pretty disgusted, but I couldn't afford to show it. Anyway, Mersey was an inoffensive chap and Calvert was a genius. I suppose I decided that you couldn't expect normal behavior from a man of his ilk.

"Gradually I got used to it, and the life was good for me. I did what I could to ease the burden on Melissa, took care of Calvert's correspondence, and the rest of the time I concentrated on my own work—God awful stuff it was too. I looked at some of it the other day, all about mortars and blood and guts. Just what you would expect from someone as unstable as I was at the time."

"What did you think of the people at the Hall?"

"As I said, Mersey was completely inoffensive. All brawn-and-looks type, but not conceited. I was fond of Melissa; she bore the brunt of everything. Calvert, well I was grateful to him but I never liked him. He was such a weak sister. You take Rosemary, for instance. Melissa made all the effort there and Calvert took all the credit. Rosemary needed the discipline that Melissa gave her, but everytime she kicked up her heels there was Calvert to play the hero and tell her it was fine. Then his sister could hunt around, find another school, and try to make it fine. That was Calvert all over."

Forsythe considered for a moment. "Rosemary came home in May, didn't she?"

"Yes, her devoted uncle instead of smacking her bottom brought her home. She did just about as she wanted, spent most of her time with Mersey. Melissa did her best to get her into a routine, interest her in war work. She did force Rosemary to help at the hospital, but Calvert kept interfering. If it hadn't been for her aunt, the girl would have been ruined."

"This is an entirely different look at Calvert," Forsythe said thoughtfully.

"Every person has many sides. However, to get back. Everything went smoothly until Vanessa Calvert decided to come back and stir things up a bit. I'd heard about Vanessa in London. The artists' colony seemed to find her affair with Calvert amusing. General idea was that after his first wife he found Vanessa too much of a challenge.

"She came to the Hall and the first time I saw her I just flipped. I'd never seen anything like her before. How Calvert could ever walk out on a woman like that—" He broke off, grinned, and reached for the bottle. "I think a drink is in order." He poured a couple of inches in both glasses and handed one to Forsythe.

"Vanessa I can describe in one word. She was a lion. Not a lioness. She was completely feminine and still a lion. Shaggy mane of red hair, slightly flattened nose, and great amber eyes.

She even moved like a lion. Swung her full weight from one foot to the other with those great shapely haunches swaying . . ."

"She seems to have made quite an impression. Would you say she was oversexed?"

Horner looked quite serious. "No. Vanessa was warm-blooded, but I think it was the effect she had on men that made people think that. Turned any man around her into a sex fiend. She turned me into one. I lusted after her. My poetry veered from battlefields to feverish works on Vanessa's thighs and breasts. I'd swear if she hadn't been four inches taller and twenty pounds heavier than I, I'd have tried to rape her."

"Did she know how you felt about her?"

"She couldn't have helped. Everytime she turned around I was panting along behind."

"What about Elinor Atlin?"

"She faded into the background. I thought at first it was just her cousin's overwhelming attraction that did it, but even when Vanessa wasn't around she was—how would you put it? Bland. But as luck would have it Vanessa wasn't interested in me. She was working on Mersey and seemed to be making no headway at all. Everytime she touched him he blushed like a girl and moved away."

"Rosemary said that Calvert didn't seem to realize what was going on, that he was the calmest one of the group."

"If he did, it certainly didn't appear to bother him. He was a thorough egotist. He adored Mersey, therefore he thought Mersey would be true to him. Calvert hadn't counted on Vanessa's charms. She didn't appear to be making much headway publicly, but she most certainly was privately.

"I know I'm not much help, Forsythe, but to be honest I must admit that except for Vanessa I didn't know another soul was alive. Maybe I'd better qualify that. I knew Melissa was going through hell. She had enough on her hands without Vanessa. Beside her war work, she had the house and Rose-mary, both big jobs. There was a maid who came in from the village and an ancient crone of a cook, but most of it fell on Melissa. She'd established a rule that the members of the household and guests must tidy their own rooms. The women were fine at this and I looked after mine army style. But you should have seen Sebastian's and Richard's. I don't think they ever did more than pull the bedspreads over their crumpled sheets and blankets."

"Did you know that Mersey and Vanessa had become lovers?"

"I certainly didn't. After the murder I found that Rosemary and Melissa had tumbled, and of course Richard set the whole thing off when he saw them. The night that he did see all was also the night that my love or lust or whatever you'd call it for the fair Vanessa vanished and was replaced by loathing."

Forsythe leaned forward, his eyes hard on Horner's face. "There was no mention of this in your testimony at the trial."

The other man's lips quirked into an ironical grin. "I'm baring my breast for you. Not much use repeating the small amount I did give at the trial. It was Thursday night, fairly late in the evening. Vanessa was in her room alone. I knew that. I'd seen Elinor talking to Melissa and Richard in the drawing room. I hunted Vanessa down in her lair, determined to throw myself bodily on her if necessary. I was really at a fever pitch and clutched a bunch of poems about her in one hot hand. Vanessa called for me to come in and there she was in one of those transparent nightgown things, brushing her hair at the dressing table.

"I can see her now, the purple chiffon not hiding one curve of her body, the brush striking sparks from that long, gorgeous hair. I more or less collapsed in a chair by the door and devoured her with my eyes. She was pretty short with me, must have been getting ready for her assignation with Mersey then.

"I got right to the point. I don't remember what I said. Probably the usual things about not being able to live without her. She just kept brushing away. Finally she lifted her head, threw back that mane of hair from her face, and yawned. Yawned, by God, like a bloody cat. Not covering her mouth or anything, just that moist red tongue curling back on her teeth.

"I must have gone wild. The next thing I knew I was behind her, my hands on her, doing my best to tear off her nightie. Vanessa was strong and had no trouble fending me off. I fell back breathing like a frustrated bull, and she calmly started to adjust a purple velvet band in her hair.

"She looked . . . amused. Finally she met my eyes in the mirror and drawled, "Go sit in your corner, little Jack Horner. Come back when you get your full growth.""

"I backed away, picked up the poems I'd thrown around, and left. I guess Vanessa always knew a person's weakest spot. She'd hit mine. I was ashamed, sensitive about my size at that time. She couldn't have found a better way to humiliate me. Anyway, I got back to my room somehow. I was close to weeping from rage. I hated her then and it was many years before I did anything else.

"I didn't sleep much that night. The following morning I intended to go and see Calvert and make some excuse to leave. But the next day, in the midst of breakfast, Calvert and Vanessa cut loose, and I figured she'd be leaving soon.

"They were really going at it, hauling all their dirty linen out, and we had to sit there and pretend we couldn't hear them. Mersey was sitting next to me. I couldn't see his face but his hands were knotted into fists. Melissa sent Rosemary upstairs and then she sat there as though turned to stone. Richard Deveraux put his hand out to pat hers and Melissa pulled her hand away in a hurry and just stared at him. Richard flushed. I didn't know he was the one who spilled the beans to Calvert. Poor Elinor kept lifting her cup but she never drank a drop. Finally it slipped out of her hand and broke on the flagstones, but nobody paid any attention. At last they finished and Calvert shouted his threat."

"He did say, 'I'll see him dead first.' "

"That's what he said, Forsythe. Then Calvert stormed up the steps to the terrace. As he passed the table he ordered Mersey to come along to his study. They left together and then Vanessa sauntered up cool as a cucumber, sat down, and helped herself to bacon and eggs. I left the table and went to a little room off the kitchen that I used as an office and tried to work."

"You didn't see any of the others for the rest of the day?"

Horner gestured toward the bottle. Shaking his head, Forsythe watched the other man refill his glass.

"I damn well didn't. I sneaked into the kitchen and got some milk and a sandwich and stayed in my room. But I couldn't get out of dinner. It was at eight as usual and Calvert joined us, which he didn't do too often. The last bit of work had been finished on his statue."

"All of you were there but Rosemary?" Horner nodded. "How did Calvert appear?"

Horner thought. "Exhilarated, almost manic. His eyes —he has the dark Calvert eyes—were glittering and he was flushed. He talked a lot and too high. Deveraux and Melissa tried to keep their end up, but the rest of us just sat there, pushing our food around on our plates. At least, all of us but Vanessa. She had a good appetite and looked like a cat lapping up cream, those amber eyes of hers sliding from Mersey's face to Calvert's.

"When Calvert dined with us we usually gathered in the drawing room later for brandy and conversation. That night we were only too eager to get away from each other. Calvert wouldn't hear of it. He asked Melissa to go up and get Rosemary and sent me down to the cellar for his most treasured wine. He had only half a dozen bottles left. I left everyone but Melissa in the dining room—she'd gone up to get Rosemary— and I went downstairs. The rest of it is in my testimony."

Forsythe consulted his notebook. "You testified that you went down, got the wine, stopped in the kitchen to open it and wipe the dust off the bottle. Then you arranged a tray, goblets and wine bottle, and carried it to the drawing room."

Taking a sip of his scotch, Horner nodded. "Right. When I got there the whole clan was gathered. I put the tray on the table near the fireplace and Calvert poured the wine. We waited for him to hand the glasses around but he didn't.

"During dinner a storm had broken, one of those fast summer storms with jagged lightning and cracks of thunder. Calvert picked up a goblet, walked to the front of the room, and pulled the drapes back. Then he started to talk. None of it made sense. He spoke in quotations about the ancient gods, the gods of thunder and lightning. We more or less milled around the table, anxious to drink up and get out. Finally Vanessa said something like, 'Well, I'm not standing here all night,' and Calvert said, 'Serve the wine.'

"Elinor was closest to the table so she handed the tray around. Sebastian gave her time to do it and when she picked up her goblet, he struck a pose in front of the window. I can still see the lightning flashing behind him. He announced he was going to propose a toast. Lifting his goblet, he called, 'To Adonis.' We all looked at Mersey. He flushed cherry red and we drank."

"You didn't notice anything odd about the taste of the wine?"

"I certainly didn't. We all more or less bolted it, anxious to have it done with and get out of there. The only ones who had any left in their goblets were Calvert and Vanessa. She stood there smiling at Calvert and then she raised her glass. 'I have another toast,' she said, 'to the victor.' Nobody moved and Vanessa raised her goblet and drained it. Calvert startled all of us. He flung his goblet and the wine in it at the fireplace. He missed and it splintered against the wall. The wine looked like spatters of blood against the ivory.

"Then Calvert turned toward Vanessa and said, 'Tomorrow I want you out of my house. Take everything you brought and go.' She was standing near Mersey. She walked over to him with that heavy, deliberate tread of hers and took his arm. She smiled at Calvert and said, 'Do you mind if I take a little more than I brought?'

"He didn't answer her, just turned on his heel and went upstairs. I was glad to see him go. It meant we could all get to our own rooms. And there was something in that room that night, a kind of . . . malevolence. You could have cut the atmosphere with a knife. Mersey went upstairs next, then Vanessa and Elinor. Melissa always locked up. She was leaning against the back of a chair and she looked ghastly, shrunken and old. She said something about locking up and Deveraux told her to go along, he'd take care of it.

"Melissa didn't argue, in fact, Rosemary had to help her up the stairs. The drug must have been taking hold. I felt dreadful, worn. It was no wonder. When the police analyzed the dregs in the wine goblets, they found we'd been fed enough barbiturates to knock out a horse.

"Deveraux was banking the fire. He looked up at me and said not to bother trying to help him, he'd look after it himself. He said I looked like hell, almost as badly as Melissa. I said something about it being no wonder after the day we'd all had.

"I left Deveraux there and went up to my room. I can't even remember getting my clothes off and falling in bed. The next morning around six—"

Forsythe leaned over and touched Horner's arm, gesturing him to silence. Then he rose, quietly covering the few feet that separated him from the door. He flung it open. Rosemary was standing there. For a moment her face was a blank. Then her lips parted and she smiled up at him. She looked much better. She'd changed her dress and put on fresh makeup.

"Oh, Robert, I was about to knock. I didn't want to interrupt you, but will you be able to stay and have tea with us? It's almost ready."

"I think not; my secretary will be waiting for me, but it was kind of you."

He started to gather up his equipment. Getting up, Horner stretched.

"Don't you want me to finish, Forsythe? It will only take a few more minutes. Rosemary can hold tea for that long."

"I don't think it necessary. You've given me what I need. The rest is covered pretty well in your testimony. We can take it from there."

The Horners walked with him to the gate. He glanced back as he left. They were standing close together, not touching. Rosemary was looking after Forsythe. Her husband's eyes were fixed on her face. Vaguely troubled, Forsythe walked toward the cab stand.

He felt tired, drained. Two things were disturbing him. He had heard Rosemary outside the shed door long before he'd moved. She'd had lots of time to knock. She wouldn't have stood there unless she was eavesdropping. And her husband's eyes had reflected an emotion that looked very much like fear.

CHAPTER 5

Forsythe's depression and weariness had vanished during the night. The following morning he worked with Miss Sanderson in their suite on the tapes of his interviews with Rosemary and John Horner. So engrossed was he that it was several minutes after one when he arrived at the Gourmet's Club. The steward directed him to a reading room and it was there that he found Richard Deveraux.

There was only one person in the room, a big man sunk in the depths of an ancient Morris chair. As Forsythe introduced himself, he was conscious of a sharp stab of disbelief. He'd expected changes in the years since a young Rosemary had sketched Deveraux, but he hadn't been prepared for the gross figure that faced him. In the bloated ruin of Deveraux's face only his eyes and hairline remained the same. The aquiline nose, firm mouth, and decisive chin had disappeared into a mass of pink flesh.

With an obvious effort, Deveraux heaved himself out of the chair.

"Do you mind if we talk after lunch, Forsythe? I've taken a lifetime membership in this club for only one reason. Come along and you'll see what I mean."

Forsythe followed him into the dining room. It was dim, paneled in dark wood. Most of the tables were occupied, but there was none of the hum of conversation that one would expect with so many diners. They seemed to be concerned only with their plates.

Lowering his bulk on a chair, Deveraux grinned at his companion. "See what I mean? The food is the whole thing. Will you have a drink before we get to it?"

"If you'll join me."

"Sorry, don't indulge anymore. My doctor's made me a promise. Unless I give up alcohol, tobacco, and cut down on food I'm not long for this world. I met him two-thirds of the way. Food, well, that's too much to expect. By the way, I've taken the liberty of ordering for you."

Their lunch arrived, served by an elderly waiter who seemed to hold his breath until he received Deveraux's nod of approval. They ate in complete silence. Forsythe could see what Deveraux meant. The cuisine was superb. He tried to avoid watching the man opposite him but at times found himself staring in fascination. Deveraux consumed literally mountains of food. His knife and fork moved like surgical instruments as he dissected lobster tails, carved pink curling slices of ham, spread sweet butter on smoking garlic bread.

After the coffee had been served, he raised his eyes to Forsythe. "Ah, that's better. Now we can get on to business. I've a couple of rooms here; gave up my house several years ago. We'll go up and do our talking in private."

A creaking lift took them to the second floor. Deveraux's living quarters were simple, a combination living and study area with a bedroom opening off it. They made themselves comfortable and Forsythe, with his host's permission, set up the recorder.

Deveraux massaged his jowl with one pudgy hand. "Now to go back, way back. I never thought I'd have to travel that road again. When I heard that Sebastian's daughter was having some digging done, I couldn't refuse to help her. But Elizabeth's wasting her time and yours."

"A few days ago, I'd have agreed with you heartily. Now, I'm not so sure. But anyway, I've taken the job on."

Deveraux looked at him quizzically, his eyes containing the touch of sardonic humour that Rosemary had caught in charcoal. "If I ask you where to start, you'll probably say the beginning. Very well. The beginning goes back to my boyhood. Don't look so alarmed, Forsythe; I'm not going to go on for hours about my youth. I only wanted to mention that Sebastian and I grew up together, went to school together. Regular Damon and Pythias relationship. We were still close in manhood. I suffered through his first marriage with him. Mary Ellen, bless her virginal little heart. Cold as ice was Mary Ellen."

Forsythe felt his lips twitch in a grin. "You sound like Rosemary. Even as a child she must have had her aunt figured."

"Rosemary was a very special child. Completely unattractive physically but with a mind like a honed razor. She learned the facts of life early. Her mother was the toast of the officers' club and the girl saw lots of action before Allan divorced his wife.

"To get back to Sebastian. We'd shared everything up to his marriage to Vanessa. Melissa was the only one who had a chance to meet Vanessa before the lovers left for Ireland. I could tell from Sebastian's infrequent letters that the woman he'd married in haste was giving him trouble. When he returned to England, he wired me to meet him at Plymouth. What a wreck got off that ship. I doubt if he could have made it to Meads Green by himself."

"Everyone has been talking around this Irish episode. Exactly what did Vanessa do to Calvert?"

Shrugging his shoulders, Deveraux said, "God knows. Sebastian was almost delirious when he arrived, raved on about the woman consuming him body and soul. Afterwards he never mentioned her again."

"But surely as his closest friend you had some idea."

"That I did. I was never under any illusions about Sebastian. I was as fond of him as one man can be of another, but I knew him. He was a man of small appetites. He complained about Mary Ellen's coldness, about every bit of love ending up in a rape scene, but I always suspected that she was an ideal wife for him. I have no idea why Sebastian was attracted to a woman like Vanessa. She had strong drives. The demands she made on Sebastian must have seemed unnatural to him. His energies were directed toward his art. I don't think he had enough left to satisfy her, so in his eyes she was a monster. A man-eating, consuming great chunk of female flesh."

"So he left her."

"Cold, and came home. He hoped never to see her again. He was like a zombie. Melissa and I were worried about him. We couldn't interest him in anything—working, recreation—nothing. Then I forced him to come to London, took him down to Limehouse to see an amateur wrestling deal. Mersey was one of the wrestlers. Sebastian sat and watched him and his eyes began to glow with the first enthusiasm I'd seen in months. When Sebastian went back to Calvert Hall, Mersey went with him."

"Did you know at that time that Mersey was a homosexual?"

"No, I didn't have a clue." Deveraux frowned. "I don't really believe at that point he was, perhaps latent but certainly not active. Mersey was a nice lad, beautifully built, a golden boy. He talked a fair amount to me about his background. Sordid business, son of a patient Griselda of a mother and a big, brawny dockworker who got drunk with great regularity and beat up his drab wife. Mersey quite obviously was devoted to his mother, loathed and feared his father. I suppose a psychologist would say that's where his tendencies came from, that he tended to identify with his mother."

Fumbling in his pocket, Forsythe located his pipe and started to fill it. "When did you tumble to the relationship between Calvert and his model?"

"My first trip to Meads Green after Mersey settled there. He'd been there about three months and the statue was really taking shape. I was delighted to see Sebastian working away with his old fervor, but I wasn't so delighted when I found out how he felt about the boy. I wasn't disgusted. Sebastian and I were in our late thirties, and I considered myself a man of the world. But I was disturbed."

"Did you try to talk to Calvert about it?"

"I did. He closed right up. Wouldn't discuss it. Said it was his business, and it was. I let it go. My hands were full at the time. My publishing business was just getting off the ground and I was involved in civil defense up to my neck."

Forsythe struck a match and held it to the pipe bowl. After a moment, he removed it from his mouth and blew out a cloud of smoke. Through it he regarded his companion's fleshy face. "Melissa asked you to help after Vanessa arrived, didn't she?"

"She phoned and told me that Vanessa had come to the Hall and she feared that Sebastian might be hurt by her again. Melissa didn't come right out and ask for me to intervene, but I knew she wanted me for moral support and also for bait."

Forsythe raised his brows. "Bait?"

"You probably wouldn't believe it to look at me now, but at that time I was considered a catch, a most eligible bachelor. A man on his way up. I wouldn't say women were falling in my path, but I had any number of chances to marry well. Melissa is a shrewd woman. She wanted Vanessa's attention diverted from Mersey and hoped I might turn the trick.

"I got to Meads Green as fast as I could. Vanessa wasn't due back until the following morning, so I had a chance to see what she had already done. Melissa was a bundle of nerves; young Horner was living in a world of his own; and Rosemary was almost out of control. Sebastian seemed glad to see me. Much to my relief, he appeared to be taking Vanessa in stride. He discussed it a bit with me and said he felt that as soon as his wife realized he wanted no more of her, she'd leave.

"I must admit that I was curious about Vanessa, looked forward to meeting her. On Monday she returned. I had never believed in love at first sight, figured it only existed in romantic novels. I changed my mind. I looked at Vanessa and knew why I had never married. My entire life must have been a waiting period for a woman like my friend's wife."

Forsythe bit down hard on his pipe. "You mean Vanessa got to you too?"

Deveraux shifted his bulk and smiled ruefully. "Got to me and stayed with me. It wasn't like John Horner's infatuation. I'm not going to say that sex wasn't connected with my feeling for her, but it was deeper than that. As you can see, it's lasted. I never married.

"Vanessa Calvert to me was a living example of the famous women who changed the course of history. For the first time I knew how Napoleon's Josephine, Cleopatra, and Helen of Troy must have appeared in the flesh. I'm not going to tell you that I couldn't see Vanessa's destructive side. She wanted to hurt Sebastian, she loved to needle him. But I believed that all she needed was the right man, someone who could handle her. I felt I was that man."

"Did Vanessa respond to you?"

An old anger moved in the depths of the other man's eyes. "She looked right through me. In a way it had the makings of a black comedy. Vanessa was in hot pursuit of Mersey; Horner was making a bloody fool of himself, sniffing after her like a fox terrier after a female Great Dane; and I was watching the whole affair, brim-up with unrequited love."

Forsythe shook his head. "She *must* be quite a woman!"

"Understatement, Forsythe. Well, that was the situation. Something was bound to give, and it did. The days passed and Thursday night arrived. I couldn't sleep. To be frank with you, I was half starved. Melissa's idea of food was pathetic. Knowing about this, I'd smuggled in my own supplies. About twelve I broke down, got out of bed, and started foraging. I had some biscuits and canned meat, so I made a rough sandwich and wandered around eating it.

"I stood by the window and looked out. It was a cloudy night, one of those nights when thick gray clouds go scudding across the moon. I glanced down into the sunken garden and at that instant the moon came popping out and I could see two people directly below. For a moment it was as clear as day. The man was Mersey and in his arms was Vanessa. They were involved in a passionate embrace. She was dressed in this sheer garment, her body was quite visible through it, and he was moving his hands over her.

"As luck would have it, clouds closed in across the moon again, and they were gone. I stood there like an idiot, my mouth full of food, not able to chew let alone swallow. I suppose I shouldn't have been hit that hard, but seeing the only woman I'd ever loved making love with another man rocked me. Even knowing it was Vanessa who had pushed the whole thing didn't help. I was wild with jealous fury, and my fury was directed at Mersey. At that moment I could have killed Adonis myself."

Deveraux paused and rubbed his eyes. "Since that night I've tried to remember exactly why I decided to face Sebastian with the truth. I couldn't sleep, in fact I didn't even go to bed. I don't think I told him for spite. I know I was wondering what would happen to his fragile balance if he stumbled over this sort of scene unwarned, whether it would be best for me to break it to him."

"So you told Calvert."

"The next morning. I went to his room. I tried to break it to him gently. Never in all the years I'd known Sebastian had I seen the look I saw that August morning. He went white and his eyes looked inhuman. He spoke calmly, even thanked me, and asked me to tell Vanessa to meet him in his study.

"I left him and headed toward Vanessa's room. I couldn't do it. I couldn't face her. I went down to the kitchen. Melissa was preparing breakfast and I told her what I'd seen, what I'd done. She stared at me. Her eyes were chips of granite. Then she said, 'I've known this, Richard, and I've been concealing it from my brother. Between Vanessa and David they've ruined him. He'll never work again.'"

Forsythe broke in. "A cold reaction from a devoted sister."

"Rather more dedicated than devoted. You must understand Melissa had carried the whole burden of the Calvert family. First Allan, then Sebastian, were the nominal heads of the family, in financial control. They never lifted a hand to look after the estate. Melissa ran it all, saw to the farms, the villagers. She'd banked all her hopes on Sebastian's genius. Even though the family ended with him, the Calvert name would be remembered." He added bitterly, "It has been remembered, but not in the way she'd hoped."

"Vanessa and Calvert didn't meet in his study, did they?"

"No. Melissa went up to Vanessa, and at first Vanessa flatly refused to get out of bed. Then she did agree to see Sebastian, but in the garden. Perhaps she wanted an audience. She loved scenes.

"While we were having breakfast, they met, and the whole thing was out in the open. I left the terrace as soon as I could, went to the drawing room and tried to read. I felt dreadfully responsible. I knew that Melissa blamed me. Time passed, and then Rosemary came running in the front door, dressed for bathing. I caught a glimpse of her face and followed her. When I got to the kitchen, she was telling Melissa about the conversation she'd overheard when Elinor Atlin was trying to persuade David not to leave Sebastian. It was clear to us that Sebastian had lost and Vanessa had won.

"Elinor came in a few minutes later and told us that Rosemary was right; it was all over. Melissa got the girl upstairs and Elinor and I persuaded Melissa to lie down in Elinor's room for a while. Melissa's iron control had given and she was close to collapse.

"The rest of the day passed in a blur. I made plans to leave the next day. I felt like a coward, but I couldn't stand any more. We managed to get through dinner and then there was the scene in the drawing room when Sebastian drugged us—"

"Just a moment." Forsythe consulted his notebook. "The drug that was used and the morphine—it was proved that everyone in the house knew of their existence and had access to them, wasn't it?"

"It was no secret. They were kept in a metal box in the medicine chest of the main bathroom. They were a carry-over from Calvert's mother. She'd died several years before of a long, painful illness. Melissa had nursed her, and they'd never disposed of the drugs that remained. Melissa, at lunch on Monday, had discussed them with her brother. She wanted to get rid of them, give them to the hospital. Sebastian agreed. We were all there."

Forsythe flipped a page in his notebook. "You were the last person downstairs on Friday night."

"I volunteered to lock up. I felt queer, but figured it was the result of the emotional binge we'd been on plus my sleeplessness the previous night. I sent Melissa to bed. Horner offered to help me, but he was looking rotten himself so I told him to turn in. I went through the house, checking the doors and windows, turning out the lights.

"By the time I got back to the drawing room, I was

stumbling. I sat down on the sofa, one of those stiff formal pieces covered in scratchy brocade. I figured I'd rest for a moment before I went upstairs. That's the last I remember. I passed out. The next morning . . ." He stopped and looked at his companion. "You know the layout of the house, don't you?"

Forsythe nodded. "I studied a sketch of it."

"The side the drawing room is on consists of two rooms. Sebastian's studio opens directly off it. Originally the studio had been a conservatory, paved in tile, with a lot of glass. Double doors, solid wood, were at the far end of the drawing room. They were closed when I went to sleep.

"When I woke up, it was just after six; I lay there trying to figure where I was. I felt as though I'd been on a six-week bash. The top of my head was coming off; my mouth tasted like a sewer; and I was stiff and sore. Then I realized that I was still in the drawing room, sprawled on the sofa. There was something over me, an afghan that generally was folded over a chesterfield at the other end of the room. Under my head was a satin cushion that was always with the afghan."

Forsythe was staring at him. "You said you passed out. If you only sat down for a minute, why did you bother with the cushion and the cover?"

Deveraux stared back. Something moved in the depths of his eyes. "I didn't. When I slumped down on the sofa both of them were in their usual place. In the night someone had put the cushion under my head and covered me up."

"This didn't," Forsythe said evenly, "come out at the trial."

"I withheld it. Only one person in that house would have been able to do it, the only person not drugged."

Without warning, Forsythe shivered. In his mind was the picture of that silent house, the occupants sleeping like the dead. Deveraux sprawled on the sofa with someone's hands lifting his head, drawing a cover over his still form.

The other man nodded with understanding. Forsythe

now recognized the expression in Deveraux's eyes. As the anger had been old, so was the fear. But it was still there. "Not a pretty thought is it, old man? A murderer stopping in the middle of his bloody work to make an unconscious man more comfortable. That's why I never mentioned it until now. It's another piece of evidence that points directly at Sebastian Calvert.

"But anyway, I came to, pushed back the afghan, and sat up, my aching head in my hands. I must have sat there for a while before I lifted my head. When I did, I saw the open doors of the studio. The weather had cleared through the night and morning sunshine slanted across the studio. Adonis was standing bathed in it, his marble body turned to gilt. I didn't waste any time looking at his beauty. I realized I was not alone. At Adonis' feet, Sebastian sat. He still wore his dinner jacket and in his arms he held something.

"I still wasn't alarmed. Getting up, I walked toward him, and then I saw what he was holding. I saw Mersey's head. It was half severed from his neck, just kind of dangling over Sebastian's arm. The body was nude and badly mutilated. Sebastian looked directly at me. Our eyes met. I saw no recognition in his. I said something, probably like, 'My God, what have you done?' He just sat there staring."

Deveraux took a deep breath. "I blanked out; I didn't know what to do. Finally I started to snap out of it. I knew I had to have help. I went up and wakened Horner. I had a devil of a time getting him conscious enough to understand me. He got up and came quietly down with me. We didn't want the women in on it.

"The little chap had a lot of guts. He took charge. He went up to Sebastian, waved his hand in front of his face. Sebastion didn't move or even blink. Horner said, 'I've seen something like this before. He won't give us any trouble; he's out of it. Better get onto the police.' Then there was this gasp behind us. It was Melissa, hanging on to the studio door. Her own eyes looked half mad. Horner managed to grab her before she collapsed. He was holding her when Rosemary started to scream. She'd followed her aunt down and saw the whole hellish thing, poor ruddy kid. Melissa pulled herself together; she had to for the girl's sake. I helped her get Rosemary out into the hall.

"They headed up the stairs and I went to the telephone. The only one in the house was in the hall, near the front door. I was talking to Sergeant Hennessy when Vanessa came downstairs, wrapped in a yellow robe. She went into the drawing room, and I finished the call. As I put down the receiver, I heard sounds of a struggle from the drawing room and Horner gasped, 'For Christ's sake, come and help.' "

"I ran in, and he was wrestling Vanessa. She was trying to get to Sebastian, had this poker in her hand. Horner couldn't begin to handle her. She was throwing him around. I grabbed her arm, but even the two of us couldn't control her. Then Elinor came from nowhere and took over. She got a hold on Vanessa and shook her. Vanessa came to her senses and started to cry. All the fight went out of her. Elinor got her into a chair and stood beside her. A few minutes later, the police and doctor got there.

"They wanted to get Sebastian out of there, someplace he could be looked after. He needed a change of clothes. The ones he had on were—well, covered. I went up to his room to get them. I was near the breaking point myself. When I opened his door all I could see was a portrait he'd done of David, a head and shoulders, in oils—magnificent. I sat down on his bed and broke right up. Gradually I pulled myself together, got up, and started automatically to straighten the bedspread again. Funny the things we do under stress. There was my best friend, directly below me, covered with the blood of an innocent boy, and what was I doing? Housework on a bed that Sebastian never slept in again."

Deveraux gestured with one hand. "That was actually

the end of it. Calvert was put temporarily into a nursing home. The doctors judged him unfit to turn up at his own trial. The evidence was weighed; Sebastian was found guilty and has spent the last twenty-five years at Grey Friar as a human vegetable. And me, well, I suppose I am eating myself to death, as my doctor says. Compensation, he calls it, a form of death wish. Sebastian killed David Mersey, but I'm just as guilty. If I'd minded my own business—"

"Calvert would have found out eventually, Deveraux. You can't blame yourself."

Deveraux didn't speak. He seemed sunk in his own thoughts.

Forsythe started to pack his recorder. Curiously, he glanced at the older man. "You weren't in the forces either. Do you mind telling me why?"

With a visible effort, Deveraux came back to the present. He touched his massive chest. "Had rheumatic fever as a lad. Left me with a wonky heart. Wasn't serious when I was younger; wouldn't be yet if I dropped some weight." He managed a grin. "We were a pretty stove-up crew at the Hall. Sebastian had a stiff knee he'd picked up in a cricket game when we were in prep school. The war had done for John Horner, and I had a heart murmur."

Snapping the lock on his case, Forsythe asked, "What about Mersey? Neither Horner nor Rosemary knew the reason he wasn't in one of the services. I suppose it was the homosexuality business that kept him out."

"Not at all. As I said earlier, I doubt whether he'd shown those tendencies until he met Sebastian. No, Mersey had a good sound medical reason. He was a diabetic."

Forsythe was on his feet, his slender form towering over the man in the chair. He shouted, "A diabetic. Do you know what you're saying, Deveraux?"

CHAPTER 6

"I don't believe it," Miss Sanderson said flatly.

Handing Forsythe a cup of tea, she shoved the plate of sandwiches closer to him. He stretched his legs toward the flickering warmth of the gas fireplace. The warmth was welcome. The sun had disappeared earlier and the late afternoon was overcast and chill.

Miss Sanderson had been working. A stack of neatly typed pages was piled on her work table beside two tapes labeled Rosemary and John Horner.

Shaking his head, Forsythe pushed the sandwich plate away. "Not after Deveraux's idea of a light lunch. You don't believe what, Sandy? No reason why Deveraux would lie about Mersey's disability."

"That's not what I meant. I don't believe a man of Deveraux's intelligence—he is intelligent, you know. He built a publishing empire that's top-rate. Surely he must have realized what Mersey's condition would have done for defense counsel. There was nothing about it in the transcript. I went over and over it."

Forsythe sipped his tea. "I suppose he didn't grasp the significance. The only people who knew that Mersey was a diabetic were Calvert and Deveraux. He said Mersey was sensitive about it, didn't want it known."

"But surely Melissa must have known. The boy would have needed a special diet, wouldn't he?"

"Deveraux vetoed that; he said Mersey just picked out what he could eat. He wasn't a large eater anyway. Melissa was much too rushed to worry about what people ate or didn't eat. As for Deveraux's intelligence—look at it fairly. It wasn't diabetes that killed the boy; it was morphine."

Miss Sanderson's jaw was set. "But the autopsy. Surely that would have disclosed it."

"Not necessarily, Sandy. If the doctors had any reason to look for it . . . certainly. But they didn't. As for the injections Mersey gave himself, well, the body was so badly mutilated they probably wouldn't show."

His companion was gently tapping her front teeth with her thumbnail. "A diabetic can die so quickly, Robby. All Calvert had to do was wait until Deveraux went back to London, empty out Mersey's insulin, and replace it with water. Sebastian could have covered the coma easily—just kept the boy in bed until he was dead. It would have looked like a natural death. No earthly reason for all the elaborate hocus pocus with barbiturates, morphine, and a scimitar." Dropping her hand, she stared at Forsythe. "Do you think that fact is enough to go on?"

Staring down into his cup, Forsythe answered slowly. "Legally, you mean, to have the case reopened? It certainly is a step in the right direction, but we'll come up against the old claim again. Calvert wasn't thinking sanely. To all intents he was a madman when he killed his model."

"Balderdash," she snorted the word. "The actual

method of murder, the morphine, was not the work of a mad mind. Wiping all the surfaces clean, does that sound like anything but a sane, logical mind? It would have been just as logical, or more so, to have let the boy die from lack of insulin."

She thought for a minute and then added, "You're right about the legal aspects. But as far as I'm concerned, this establishes Calvert's innocence. I would suppose we can also eliminate Deveraux. He could have killed Mersey the same way."

Forsythe sat up. "I disagree. Deveraux was a guest in the house. He wouldn't have had the same chance to cover Mersey's death. And Calvert was there, close to the boy. He knew all about the body's condition. No, Deveraux is still very much in the running."

"Well . . ." She sighed deeply, pulled herself from her chair, and walked over to her work table. "I guess we might as well continue digging. "Oh." She stopped suddenly and turned toward Forsythe. "There are two messages for you. Our client must be becoming impatient. Wants you to meet her this evening. Here it is, time and place." She handed him a slip of paper. "She picks a queer spot for a business appointment, doesn't she?"

Forsythe glanced at the address. "That she does, but she's paying the bills. I'll have to humor her." He looked up at his secretary. "You said two, what's the other?"

Miss Sanderson's face was cold. "Better brace yourself. After all these years, the lily maid of Astolat wants to see you. She's staying at the Stewart Arms."

Sticking the slip of paper into his pocket, Forsythe reached for the telephone. Her eyes bleak, his secretary watched.

"Are you actually going to contact her?"

"Why not?"

She sat down in front of her typewriter and began to roll a sheet of paper into it. "Indeed, why not?" She added, "She has the pound of flesh, why not the blood?"

Forsythe was dialing. He didn't appear to hear her. Miss Sanderson started pounding the keys as though she was punishing the machine.

When he stepped through the door of the cocktail lounge, Virginia was the first person he saw. She sat at a small corner table, the light from the centerpiece illuminating her face.

She hadn't changed. Sandy's nickname, "the lily maid of Astolat," suited her. Virginia's beauty was pastel, all pale gilt hair and cameo face. Her figure was curved and faintly sensual. Forsythe waited for the familiar leap of his heart. It didn't come.

When he reached her side, she raised her head. Her voice was the same also, low and husky. "It was good of you to come, Robert. You haven't changed."

"I was just thinking the same about you. It's been a long time."

She nodded, sheaves of pale hair swinging against her face. "Five and a half years. I've never tried to see you. Guilty feelings, I guess, for what I've done to you."

"You did nothing to me, Virginia. Anything that happened was my own decision."

Her eyes dropped. He studied the shadow the fringe of lashes cast on her cheeks. A waitress in a brief skirt and a low-cut blouse took their order. When it was delivered, Virginia lifted her eyes and her glass.

"Perhaps I phrased it badly. I meant I feel responsible. I did a foolish, panicky thing. Bribing Jennings to change his testimony. But I was young, Robert, and afraid. All I could see was the mound of evidence against me and the death penalty if I was found guilty."

Forsythe put his glass down. "So young, so frightened, so lacking in faith. I would have got you off. I could have proved that a prowler entered your house that night. With the witnesses I had lined up to show your husband's wild temper, it's probable they would have found the shooting a result of the entry."

Virginia shuddered. "Frank was a terrible man. I can't believe I actually lived three years with him."

"And now, are you happy?"

"Very. We have a son, three years old. I know I should have told you before our wedding, but Douglas wanted no one to know. There was so much publicity because of the trial."

"I can see what he meant." Fishing in his pocket, Forsythe's fingers touched his pipe and then fell away from it. "Graham's name had been linked with yours."

Her eyes met his. They were glittering, luminous, as though with unshed tears. "Douglas and I owe you so much, Robert. You were the only one who seemed to believe in my innocence."

"Much more," he said gently, "than you believed in my ability."

"You protected me. When the rumors started circulating, you left your practice so they wouldn't know it was—"

"I loved you."

Her expression was distressed. "I know. I wish I had loved you. I couldn't, even after all you did for me."

"You can't control love. However, enough about the past. What did you wish to see me for?"

"Just to see you. I was in London and heard that you were here too. You never seem to leave your home. I was wondering . . . " Her voice trailed off.

There was compassion in his eyes. "I haven't come to resume my practice. It's an entirely private matter that brought me here."

She tossed the gilt hair back from her face. "I'm incredibly selfish, Robert. It's Douglas and my son. I don't know how I could face any more."

Pushing back his chair, he answered the question in her eyes. "I gave you my word."

She put one slim hand over his. "Would you care to have dinner with me?"

He glanced at his watch and rose. "I'm sorry. I won't even have time for a sandwich. I've an appointment and I'll be late if I don't hurry."

"Perhaps we can see each other before I leave. You could ring me."

"I'll try." He touched her shoulder. "Goodbye, Virginia."

He was conscious of her eyes following him as he left. He didn't look back.

It was twilight when Forsythe turned on to Fish Hill Street. He hadn't been wholly truthful with Virginia. He'd not been late. There had been time to walk from Stewart Arms to the Monument.

He saw it looming ahead of him against the darkening sky. The silhouette of the vase of flames at the very top caught the last weak rays of light. He cast only a glance at the bas-relief of the City of London as he passed it. For almost three hundred years the mournful woman representing London after the Great Fire had drooped in the same position, ignoring the other figures attempting to raise her.

Forsythe gave the guardian a good evening and his sixpence and started up the winding black marble steps. He blessed the sports that had kept his wind sound as he reached the two hundredth step. At step three hundred, he began to wonder whether he *had* kept himself in good shape.

All this was forgotten as he stepped into the iron-grilled cage at the Monument's top. For a moment he glanced down at the sweeping view of domes, roof tops, chimney pots, and winding streets.

After a moment, he realized he wasn't alone. At the east end a small figure dressed in cloak and hood stood silently.

"Elizabeth?" he called.

Without turning her head, she spoke. "The view is worth that awful climb, isn't it? This is the first time I've been up here. Uncle Howard said my mother loved this view when she was a young girl."

Joining her, he looked down at the Tower and the Thames, wide and silver, running beneath its many bridges toward Westminster. Mist was rolling in eerie grey billows from the river.

"It looks as though we may be in for a spot of fog. A bit unseasonal." He looked at his companion. All he could see was her profile, the thin proud nose, her eyes veiled by her lashes.

"I've been waiting," she said abruptly. "Sitting around that dreadful little apartment waiting. Do you have anything yet?"

"I've been able to speak with the prosecutor, Sir Hilary Putham, and I've managed to get the full brief from Peter Meredith. Three of the witnesses, Deveraux, Rosemary, and John Horner, have been interviewed."

"Were they willing to be interviewed?"

"Yes. Rosemary and Deveraux did their best. Horner, well he came around. By the way, Elizabeth, your cousin said you hadn't contacted her."

"I haven't. Have you uncovered anything, Robert, that will help?"

He shifted his position, trying to see her face more clearly. "There are a couple of things," he said cautiously. "Nothing concrete, but something to start with. I think I can safely say that my secretary and I have no doubt that there was a miscarriage of justice. We feel your father is innocent."

"Will it stand up in court?" He shook his head. Her voice rose slightly. "If Sebastian Calvert is innocent, one of the other six must be guilty. Have you any idea which one?"

Again his head moved in a negative gesture "It's still too

early. I have the other three to talk with—Vanessa, Melissa, and Elinor. This is a matter of patience. A murderer who has managed to stay concealed for all these years is not going to be easy to flush out in the open."

She wheeled to face him. In the dark shadow of her hood he could see the glitter of her eyes, the set of her mouth. "I'm expecting too much, too soon, but it seems so—hopeless. How can you force a confession from a person who would hide the truth, allow me to suffer the way I've suffered?"

He spoke mildly. "Your cousin has suffered and so, I imagine, has your Aunt Melissa."

"To hell with their suffering. They had a part of him, a share of his life. They've earned their suffering. I haven't. One of them might even have killed Mersey."

He walked away from her to a point where he could see the dome of St. Paul's. Her voice followed him.

"I'm sorry, Robert. I'm afraid I don't make a good waiter. I'm on edge tonight. You're doing well, at least you feel there is a chance. Where do you go from here?"

"To Rome. Vanessa has lived there for a number of years. I leave in the morning."

He hadn't heard her move but he felt her hand on his arm.

"Please keep me informed. If it's a matter of money—"

"I don't think there's anyone or anything we can buy, Elizabeth."

Her hand fell away and she turned back to her study of London.

He regarded her steadily. The feeling of unease she seemed to induce troubled him. After a moment he moved away from her, toward the steps.

"Are you coming down now, Elizabeth? I'll see you back to your apartment."

"No." Her voice was muffled. "I think I'll stay here a little longer. You go along."

He went down the corkscrewing steps past the guardian. Crossing King William Street, he halted in front of Monument station. Vainly he tried to hail a cab. It was cold now and dark. The fog he had predicted was rolling in. Finally, he shrugged, turned up his coat collar, and prepared to walk back to his hotel.

It was an eerie walk. There weren't many pedestrians and they loomed suddenly from the fog, upon him before he realized they were there. He strode along swiftly. A few blocks from the hotel, Forsythe decided to leave the main thoroughfare and shorten his time by cutting down a quiet, cobblestoned street. The fog seemed lighter here, drifting in swirls. He passed the shop fronts, most of them shuttered for the night.

Toward the end of the street he could make out the street light on the corner where he would turn. He lengthened his stride, eager to be out of the clammy fog. He'd almost reached the corner when he stumbled. As he fought for his balance he heard it. The soft rush of footsteps behind him and then a sharp crack. At the same instant, he felt the blow, searing pain along the left side of his head.

Breaking into a run, he covered the distance left and fell into the side door of his hotel. Pulling himself to a stop, he stood there panting. In the mirror over the desk he could see himself. His face was white and tense. A dribble of blood was running down his cheek.

His shock was mirrored in the face of the man behind the desk.

"Mr. Forsythe. You've been hurt."

The desk clerk hurried around the desk, his hand out. Forsythe waved him away. Pulling out his handkerchief, he pressed it against the side of his head.

"Just a scratch. Ran into a lamppost in the fog. Clumsy."

"Think you should have it looked at, sir? I could ring up a doctor. There's one just around the corner."

Forsythe managed a reassuring smile. "It's not that serious. I'll go up and dab something on it. Good night."

He was aware of the man's worried eyes on him as the lift door closed.

Miss Sanderson's eyes were on her work. She was typing, a cigarette held in her mouth, one eye closed against the smoke. She looked tired.

"Back so soon, Robby? There's coffee on the table. It's still hot." She glanced up. The cigarette fell from her lips unheeded. "My God! You're covered with blood."

She was on her feet. Forsythe allowed her to push him into a chair. She tilted his head up to the light. "Looks worse than it is. Just a shallow groove along your skull. What in hell have you been doing?"

"Minding my own business. Walking along and someone took a shot at me. Just outside the hotel. Luckily I stumbled over a cobblestone at the same time."

She straightened. "Are you sure?"

He dabbed at his face. "I know a gun when I hear one. Better get something and clean me up a bit."

She was only gone a minute. The tin box she brought back had a small red cross on one side. Her hands were deft.

"This will sting."

He winced. It did. She stood back and surveyed her work.

"You look piratelike with that sticking plaster on your head. Quite dashing."

Forsythe grinned up at her, but her concerned expression didn't change.

"Looks as though the digging you're doing has upset someone. You've received your warning."

"If I hadn't stumbled, old dear, I'd be out there with a neat hole in the middle of my head. That was no warning. Whoever dislikes me meant it for keeps."

Gently her nail flicked her tooth. "But what for? We

haven't anything definite." She lowered her hand and started to count on her fingers. "Rosemary Horner listening at a door she could just have opened and entered. A look that you swear was fear in John Horner's eyes. Deveraux's claim that the murderer took time to cover him up. The knowledge that Mersey was a diabetic. Just a bunch of unconnected facts."

"Apparently someone is afraid we'll connect them, Sandy. Even after all these years we must be on a hot trail. Maybe someone said too much and didn't realize it at the time. Perhaps one of the people we haven't yet interviewed fears something that John, Rosemary, or Richard could have told us."

"The burning question right now is—do you continue?"

His mouth was suddenly grim. "Nothing could stop me now."

She returned his look. "A bullet might."

"Let it go for now, Sandy. Do you have my reservation for Rome tomorrow?"

Her hands were busy with the coffee pot. Handing her companion a steaming cup, she flicked the gas fire up a notch and sank into a chair opposite him.

"All in order. You must be looking forward to meeting Vanessa Calvert. From those comments on the tapes, she's something of a puzzle. The effect she made on the people who knew her is confusing. How can one woman be all those things?"

"I know what you mean, Sandy. Goddess, natural force, lion. Definitely a woman of many parts."

Miss Sanderson grinned. "You've forgotten Deveraux. Blimey, Helen of Troy and Josephine wrapped up in one package. However, Robby, twenty-five years is a long time. Don't be disappointed if Vanessa is no longer the package she once was."

He smiled back at her. "Goddesses and natural forces know no age."

"Lions do, my boy. They get mangy hides and lose all their teeth. Then," she looked gloomily into the fire, "the hyenas gather to finish them off."

They sat in silence for a while. Finally Miss Sanderson lifted her eyes and looked hopefully at her companion. "Any chance of changing that single reservation into a double? I could go along as a kind of bodyguard."

He chuckled. "Guarding me from what—bullets or Vanessa?" He said to Miss Sanderson, "I'm sorry."

CHAPTER 7

Forsythe said to Vanessa Calvert, "I'm sorry."

"You should be. You were *staring*. But don't look so abashed, Mr. Forsythe; I should be used to it by now. In a way I suppose I even like it. I would far rather be stared at than ignored. Tell me, do you find me a disappointment?"

Forsythe would have liked to have avoided that question. He'd felt a sharp stab of regret when he'd first seen her. She was sitting under a peppermint-striped awning at a tiny glass-topped table. The Italian sunlight was merciless. Vanessa was still impressive, but the flesh on her upper arms was loose and the breasts that John Horner had immortalized in poetry were pendulous. Under the broad brim of a white hat, her hair was an improbable shade of red, quite frankly dyed. Huge sunglasses obscured her eyes and features. It was when she had removed them that Forsythe had stared. The essence of the Vanessa he'd heard about still lived, mirrored in huge amber eyes.

He saw the same amusement that the people he'd talked with had remembered.

"Don't bother answering that question. You'll probably try to be tactful and I loathe tact." She sipped her liqueur. "I must admit that after the trial many of the stares directed at me were unfriendly. They say one can't touch pitch without being dirtied with it. It's true. The most unholy rumors have come to my ears through the years. Not only about myself. I could understand that. But the gossips spared no one. Poor Melissa was painted as some sort of middle-aged monster who procured innocent young men for her depraved brother. Sebastian's relationship with his niece, Rosemary, was bandied about. Even his friendship with Richard was hinted at being unnatural. They decided that John Horner, one of the most masculine men I've ever known, was another of Sebastian's lovers. Bloody nonsense, all of it."

"What did you hear about yourself?"

She moved one white-clad shoulder. "Another monster, crazed with sex, who had nearly driven Sebastian mad during our marriage and finished the job by luring David away from him. In my case they did have some grounds, though I never considered that Sebastian had to be driven to it. He was always unbalanced, couldn't quite stand women."

"He did marry twice."

"And both were flaming successes, weren't they?"

Forsythe tried another tack. "Do you mind me coming here, rehashing past history?"

"Mind? No, I'd say the reverse. It's been a deadly dull season. If you wish to waste your money, or I suppose I should say Sebastian's daughter's money, it's fine with me."

"There's no use of asking you how you feel about your husband's guilt, is there?"

"Not the slightest. You said you've read my testimony. It still stands. Sebastian couldn't face the fact that David preferred a woman to him. I think I might have understood him killing the boy, but I couldn't understand how he could chop that magnificent body to bits. What a build the lad had. Now the battle lines are drawn, Mr. Forsythe. You understand I have nothing to contribute to clear my dear husband's name. Do you have any questions?"

Forsythe signaled the waiter for another drink. He was a good looking chap, hirsute, but with fine eyes. His manner was a blend of contempt and servility. Forsythe noticed he managed to brush against Vanessa. She didn't draw away.

"Questions, yes. Why did you return to your husband's home if you disliked him so intensely?"

"Not disliked. I don't like; I adore. I don't dislike; I hate. I hated Sebastian. Not at first. I think I fell in love with his work, with the fine, passionate things he created. I confused the art with the man. It wasn't long before I found that he was a spineless mass with ice water in his veins. But in my own way I did everything possibly to make our marriage work. Sebastian was unique. Not only was he the only man I ever married but also the only one to walk out on *me*. It wasn't with any thoughts of patching our marriage up that I came to the Hall. It was a simple matter of money."

Forsythe raised his brows. "I understood that you were wealthy in your own right."

"On paper I was. At that time the principal was still in trust and I had only an allowance to live on. It was generous, but I lived on rather an exalted scale. What I wanted I bought. On the black market you could get anything you desired. But it was expensive. I was stony broke. I'd never asked anything from Sebastian, so I decided he might as well divvy up."

"Calvert wasn't a mean man. Why didn't you write and ask him for some help?"

She lifted her glass in a large, shapely hand. "You don't know me. I wanted him to ask me to accept it. I thought after a few days in his peaceful home he'd be willing to bribe me to leave. I didn't have the faintest idea about David. The moment

I saw him all idea of money was gone. I'd have wanted him even if he hadn't belonged to Sebastian. That only added spice to the chase."

"And you won first prize, Mrs. Calvert?"

"Won and lost. David chose me and Sebastian killed him. It's as simple as that."

"Did you know that David Mersey was a diabetic?"

She frowned. "No, I didn't. Was he really?" She looked at Forsythe sharply. "What is this supposed to mean to me?"

"Calvert knew. Doesn't it seem strange that he killed the boy the way he did?"

"Not at all. It's the old story of Salome all over again. She wanted John the Baptist's head. Calvert wanted me to have David served up like a butchered carcass of beef. The man was mad, Mr. Forsythe, mad. At the trial I'll admit I thought he was faking, trying to escape punishment. I know better now."

"I see." Forsythe's eyes moved from Vanessa's face to the people sauntering along the street. Many of the girls were lovely, moving with a sensuous grace. His dark suit felt out of place. In the brassy sunlight of Rome, among its bright colors, he felt stiff, very English, and depressed. He'd wasted his time. Vanessa had nothing for him.

Vanessa's voice called him back. "I am what I am. I'm not going to say I'm a perfect human being. I'm merely human. I didn't seek Sebastian out to do him harm. I loved David, wanted him. The loss of that beautiful, bright creature was painful. You've seen the *Adonis?*"

"I've seen it. I've also seen the love that Calvert put into it."

"Love of one man for another. What kind of love is that?"

"I don't sit in judgment, Mrs. Calvert, and try to decide what is right and what is wrong. All I know is that the emotion in that piece of stone is as pure as any emotion that the human beings you were mentioning are capable of. That's why it will outlive our lives, our time. Long after Mersey's death is forgotten, Sebastian Calvert's love will immortalize his *Adonis.*"

"A pretty sentiment, but only empty words. The model is dead."

Forsythe started to rise. Then he sank back into his chair. "I almost forgot. Neither Elizabeth's investigator or my own bloodhound, Miss Sanderson, was able to trace your cousin. Can you tell me where I can find her?"

Vanessa looked directly at him. He couldn't read the expression in the golden eyes. "Lin? I suppose they might have drawn a blank. Yes, I can tell you where she is, but it won't help you."

"Will she not be willing to speak with me?"

"No, Lin will not speak with you. There's a tiny village in the Swiss Alps called by the unbelievably trite name of Edelweiss. On the mountain behind the village there's a deep crevice. At the bottom of it is Lin. She's been there for twenty years."

"But we couldn't find any record of her death."

"The record is there in the little town hall, all spelled out neatly on a brass plaque. It mentions such words as gallantry, bravery. It doesn't say anything about stupidity. It should."

"How did she die?"

"Lin left me shortly after the trial. We'd been together as long as I can remember. Her parents died when she was young of some type of jungle fever in a godforsaken outpost. They were medical missionaries. I was an only child, and my parents raised Lin as my sister. She was much like her parents, an idealist, very religious. I don't know how she stood me. She disapproved of me completely. But there was a bond, a strong one, between us. The only time we were ever apart was the year I spent in Ireland.

"Lin didn't want me to go to the Hall, but she never could stop me. She was a bit of a martyr. I said she needn't come, but she tagged along anyway. When we got there and the ruckus started over David, she sided with Melissa and the rest. After the first few days, she gave up trying to reform me. But even at the end, the Friday when Sebastian had it out with me, Lin went to David and tried to convince him he'd be better off with Sebastian. She told him I'd give him a rotten time."

"After the trial Miss Atlin left you."

"Couldn't bear the sight of me. Lin blamed me for the whole grisly business. I never realized until she was gone how much I depended on her. I've missed her. But to get to her death. Lin had no money of her own; her parents left her nothing. As the saying goes, they were as poor as church mice. She took a job as a governess; a Swiss banker hired her. She was on vacation when she died, a skiing holiday. A boy had fallen in the crevasse. Only his father and brother were on the mountainside. They didn't know what to do. The child had been caught partway down on an outjutting of ice. He was hanging there, unconscious. Lin knew there was no time to get more help; the ice might collapse at any moment. She roped herself up and went down after him. There was only one rope. She tried to make a noose, get it around him. She found the rope wouldn't support both their weights.

"So Lin got a toehold on the ice, got the rope off herself and around him. They got the boy up all right. They were just lowering it to her when the ice gave. They said she didn't make a sound as she fell."

Forsythe stared at the woman. "You call that stupid."

She waved a hand wearily. "The boy died that afternoon in the hospital of internal injuries. She'd given her life for a child who was to all intents already dead."

"She never knew that."

"No, Lin never knew."

There was a pause. Then Forsythe did get up.

Vanessa raised mocking amber eyes. "I wasn't any help to you, was I?"

His voice was even. "You never intended to be."

She gave him a smile, her lips curling back from even white teeth. "Goodbye, Mr. Forsythe, I shan't wish you good luck."

He strode away. His shoulders, under the dark jacket, were erect. She watched his slim figure vanish in the crowds. The waiter was back, one hand on her shoulder.

"Tonight, Signora? The usual place."

She glanced at his hand, her eyes icy. "Haven't you learned yet, Giulio? I do the touching."

He withdrew his hand but didn't move away. After a moment she snapped her sunglasses into place. Behind them her eyes traveled up the column of his throat to his heavy jaw.

She shrugged and reached for her glass. "Tonight, Giulio. Why not?"

CHAPTER 8

Shifting slightly, Melissa Calvert paused, her hands hovering over the tea tray.

"Milk or lemon? Yes, here you are. Do have a scone; they're delicious. I can say that honestly as I didn't bake them. I've always been a poor cook and now I rely mainly on bakeshops for this sort of thing." She took a tiny sip of her own tea and regarded her guest. "I must admit, Mr. Forsythe, I was surprised to hear that you'd met Vanessa only two days ago. You don't wear that dazed expression that Vanessa usually induces in males."

"It's been a long time since you've seen her. She's aged but I could still see a hint of the magic she once must have had."

"I've never been able to picture her as any different than she was in forty-four. Other people, yes, I have no trouble associating them with age. Not poor Vanessa."

Forsythe raised his brows and studied his companion. Sir Hilary had been correct. The plain woman was now stunning. Her dark hair had turned into silver plaits, drawn around

features softened and beautified by time. Only her eyes, dark
and flashing behind heavy-rimmed glasses, reminded him of the
sketch made by Rosemary Horner. He questioned Melissa.
"Poor?"

She smiled faintly. "It must sound strange to you when
I use a word of that type with Vanessa's name. But I've never
really disliked her even though I know that she was directly
responsible for my brother's ruin. I've always pictured Vanessa
as something of, now what is the word? The mischievous ghosts
who rattle and bang—"

"Poltergeist," Forsythe suggested.

"That's the word. A big troublemaking child in a
woman's attractive body."

"A dangerous combination."

"Perhaps not to the average man. To my brother, yes.
He should never have married at all." She smiled at the expression on Forsythe's face. "Spinsters are reputed to be innocent,
dried up creatures with no comprehension of life. I'm afraid
that's a fallacy. The mere fact that they have no life of their
own, live in other people's lives, makes then see more accurately
than the people involved.

"Sebastian was not masculine. His first marriage to
Mary Ellen Pennell was the result of my interference. Good
intentions do pave the way to hell. I very much wanted an heir,
a son to carry on the Calvert line. Allan was no help. He had
a daughter, Rosemary, but his marriage was breaking up. So I
forced my younger brother into a marriage he didn't wish.

"I thought Mary Ellen would be ideal for Sebastion. She
came from a fine background and seemed a quiet, competent
girl. I was being selfish to an extent. The estate had been my
responsibility for so long that I hoped she might be able to take
over. I was over thirty and felt time slipping away from me."

"His marriage didn't work out as you had hoped."

"Not in any way. I only gained another burden. Sebastian was unhappy and as for Mary Ellen . . . she did put in an

appearance at social gatherings, garden parties and fêtes, posing in flowered chiffon and large floppy hats. Other than that she did nothing. Mary Ellen was much addicted to lounges and people waiting on her. She became pregnant, and I was overjoyed. But her conduct became worse. I sometimes have felt if she had moved around a bit she might still be alive."

"She wasn't a delicate woman?"

Melissa snorted. It reminded Forsythe of Sandy's derisive sound. "Far from it. The doctor tried to make her exercise, but she actually died of complications that could happen to any woman in childbirth. Sebastian was, I think, inwardly relieved. He set about getting rid of the baby as fast as possible. I wanted to keep Elizabeth, raise her as my own child, but he wouldn't hear of it. He wanted no reminder of his wife. So Howie and Anne Pennell took her. It worked out better for the child. At least she was spared a certain amount. I'd hoped she would never have to know about her father. But Howie must have decided otherwise."

"A wise decision, Miss Calvert. Elizabeth was bound to have learned sometime, the shock . . ."

Melissa didn't appear to be listening. She was looking down at her knee. Her composure was much better than Rosemary's had been. Any disturbance she felt was betrayed by her hands. One of them was nervously pleating the silk of her dress, Elizabeth's gesture.

"Knowing Sebastian as I did, I was amazed to learn that he planned to remarry. He met Vanessa in London, at a cocktail party, and within a month they were married. He did bring her to the Hall first to meet me. I was dismayed when I saw her, saw that robust, demanding nature of hers. I tried to persuade both of them to wait, at least for a short while. This was one time I couldn't sway Sebastian. He wouldn't even wait for Richard Deveraux to meet her. Well, you must know about that. When Sebastian returned, I tried to build him up, get him back to work . . ."

She looked up at Forsythe, met his eyes squarely. "Many close friends feel I was interested in Sebastian the artist to the exclusion of Sebastian the brother. At one time I would have denied this. But as one gets older one has a tendency to lose self illusions. My brother was not an admirable man. He was weak, vain, and unbelievably selfish. But he was also a great artist. I was glad when he brought David home even though I sensed immediately that Sebastian's interest in him was homosexual. If anyone was corrupted, it was young David. But he was easily corrupted. His parents had died a short time before—"

"Deveraux told me," Forsythe interrupted, "that Mersey came from a sticky home, wife beating and all that."

"He did. His father had beaten his mother once too often. She died of her injuries. In drunken remorse the man killed himself. David considered his mother a saint. But, as I said, he was alone, no education, a slum product. Sebastian changed all that and David liked the changes. He was a protégé of a rich and famous man, living at the Hall. His future was assured. I have called him a chameleon. He was. When he found what Sebastian wanted from him, he went along with it. And, God forgive me, so did I. If David had been a true homosexual I doubt whether Vanessa would ever have swayed him."

Forsythe looked at his notebook. "Rosemary returned in the spring and then in August Vanessa and Elinor Atlin arrived."

"Yes, Rosemary came home. I'd accepted David and although I wasn't happy about Rosemary being at the Hall, I accepted that also. David and Sebastian were discreet. I never believed that the child would understand what their true relationship was. Rosemary was always clever. She hid her knowledge from me and life went on.

"I was overworked. I suppose you've heard about that. It was my own fault, but I felt it necessary. Our country was at war. You've probably also heard about my stand on our rations. I was teased about it, but I felt this necessary too. Thousands of others were getting by and we would also. Rosemary still complains about it. The truth is that it was good for her. Her skin was bad and she was overweight."

She paused. "If you don't mind waiting, I'll make some fresh tea. I find it soothing. Excuse me."

Forsythe watched her leave the room. He liked Melissa Calvert. There was a physical resemblance to Elizabeth, and Melissa used the same pleating motion. Other than that, he noticed no similarity to her niece. Melissa was a strong woman, honest and possibly ruthless, but she made no effort to spare herself. In a way she reminded him of Sandy.

He looked around the room. It was a compact flat, modern and comfortably arranged, but looking more like a hotel suite than a home. The only touch that indicated Melissa's background was a delicate Sheraton desk near the window. There were few ornaments and no photographs.

She wasn't gone long. Pouring out hot tea, she started to speak.

"When Vanessa and Elinor arrived, I knew immediately what was going to happen between my sister-in-law and David. I saw her eyes when he came into the drawing room in his bathing outfit. Even knowing didn't help. I was powerless to stop her. For a time I had hopes; David seemed to be fending Vanessa off. But I felt her undoubted appeal would eventually break him down. In desperation I called Richard. Women liked him. I thought Vanessa might take to him."

"Just the opposite happened, Miss Calvert."

"Richard fell in love with her. I couldn't believe it. He'd had a great deal of experience with women, but I'd never seen him lose his head. Even Richard was no help.

"Then the Wednesday night before the tragedy, my fears were confirmed. I saw Vanessa leaving David's room. I pushed Rosemary behind me, hoping vainly that she wouldn't see. Then I closed my eyes and stood there wondering what I could do. Rosemary was upset, so I took her to our bedroom and told her to go to sleep.

"I waited a moment to see that she was all right and then I went to Vanessa's room. I was in a rage. I didn't bother knocking, just flung open the door and marched right in. Vanessa was in bed, propped up on her pillows. The upper part of her body was wrapped in her spare blanket. She always had her window wide open. She was calmly reading a novel and eating chocolates. Black-market, no doubt."

Forsythe stifled a grin at this point. Melissa didn't notice. Her hand was busily pleating again.

"Vanessa looked up and asked me why I had come at that ungodly hour and couldn't I knock. I said to her, 'Don't play games with me, Vanessa; you know why I'm here. I saw you coming from your rendezvous with David. My niece saw you too. This is too much. This is as much my home as Sebastian's. I want you to leave.' "

"She did have grace enough to drop her eyes. When she looked up, they were glowing with unholy amusement. The woman had no shame, no decency. She did look lovely. That mass of hair, held back with a green satin ribbon, was spilling over the blanket.

"She said quite softly, 'Would you rather that Rosemary caught her beloved uncle coming out of David's room?' I didn't answer. I couldn't. I was choked with rage." Melissa stopped abruptly and looked at Forsythe. "I have never understood why David was killed and not Vanessa. If ever a woman could inspire murder, it was her. But to get back. She threw her hair back and smiled at me. 'Very well,' she said, 'I know when I'm not welcome. I'll leave quietly, but of course I'll have to tell Sebastian the reason.' "

"Vanessa knew she had the upper hand. At that time I had no idea how close Sebastian's statue was to completion. I needed time. She read my face and laughed. 'We'll be fellow conspirators, Melissa. You keep my secret and I'll keep it too.' She'd won. All I could do was swing on my heel and leave."

"You didn't gain much time, Miss Calvert."

"I blamed Richard for years. But it would only have postponed it if he hadn't told Sebastian. My brother would have found out. Vanessa loved to torture him; she'd have told him herself.

"Friday morning Richard told me my secret was no longer a secret, that Sebastian knew and wanted to see Vanessa. I went up to her. She wouldn't agree to go to Sebastian's study. She said he might have everyone else on a string but she'd broken hers. They met in the sunken garden. I suppose you know exactly what happened."

"Yes, that's been well covered. Could you tell me something about the rest of the day? Where was everyone and what were they doing? I know it's expecting a lot from your memory—"

"My memory is clear, Mr. Forsythe. I've often wished it wasn't. After breakfast Rosemary came bolting in and told me that David had chosen Vanessa. She was overwrought. It was hard enough for an adult in that house, but a child exposed to the tension . . . Well, I put her to bed, and Richard and Elinor insisted I rest in Elinor's room so I wouldn't disturb Rosemary. As I started upstairs, David was just returning from the lake. He came in the front door, brushed past me without a word, and went up to his room. As I passed his door, I heard the lock click. He stayed there until dinner time.

"I couldn't stay still. In a short time I got up and went downstairs. All was quiet. Richard was in the drawing room reading. John Horner was in a little room at the back of the house where he worked. Rosemary, of course, remained in our room. The cause of all the trouble was on the terrace. Vanessa was stretched out in a chaise lounge, sleeping quite peacefully in the sun. Sebastian was in his studio."

"Was that the situation until dinner time?"

"That was it. I went down to the kitchen and Elinor joined me there. We did housework; we didn't bother with lunch. Everyone was busy staying as far away from the others as possible. I don't know how I would have gotten through the day without Elinor."

"What was your opinion of Elinor, Miss Calvert?"

"I think perhaps I tended to identify with her. She was in somewhat the same position as I. Elinor saw her cousin with harsh realism. She knew that Vanessa was completely amoral, but Elinor was devoted to her. Their separation during my brother's marriage had been a sore blow for Elinor. I think that Elinor feared that Vanessa and David would have no room in their lives for her. I believe that was the reason she entreated David to stay with Sebastian. None of our actions are wholly selfless. But whatever the reason, Elinor was one note of sanity in that dreadful August."

"Can you tell me about dinner that night?"

"Elinor cooked it. I puttered around in the kitchen, made the coffee. It was even worse than usual. We arranged a tray for Rosemary and I took it up to her while Elinor put the dinner on the table. Dinner itself was awful. Richard and I did our best to act as though nothing had happened. The rest, except for Sebastian, didn't try."

"How did Sebastian strike you, his behavior at dinner?"

"Frankly, he frightened me. He was excited, spots of color on his cheekbones and his eyes flashing. He seemed frightfully keyed up."

"You hadn't expected this reaction."

"With Sebastian, of course, you could never be certain. But I had thought he would be quiet, draw in on himself. He was the opposite." Her fingers were working at her skirt again. "I suppose he was breaking down even then, nerving himself to do the horrible thing he did later that night."

"There is no doubt in your mind that your brother did kill Mersey?"

"I've struggled through the years to believe otherwise. It's been an impossibility. I was there, you see; it could have been no one else. You think me a poor sister not to share Rosemary's belief in Sebastian's innocence? Well, there was the matter of the drugged wine—"

"Just one moment, Miss Calvert." This time Forsythe didn't check his notebook. "John Horner brought the wine from the cellar. He opened the bottle in the kitchen. Surely he had the same opportunity."

"There was no trace of mother's barbiturate in the bottle. The only traces they found were in the goblets. We all put them down just anywhere when we went to bed."

"I know that. But Horner could have put the drug in the goblets *before* the wine was poured. He arranged the goblets on the tray."

"It wasn't brought out at the trial, Mr. Forsythe, but the drug itself was a liquid, pale brown. The goblets were clear crystal. Even a small amount would have shown. Someone would have noticed it."

"After Sebastian poured it, he didn't serve it immediately. I see the rest of you were 'milling around the table.'"

"We were. Most of the others were watching Sebastian. I wasn't. I couldn't bear to look at him because he disturbed me to such a degree. I was close to the table. I'd swear that no one had a chance to pour the liquid into the wine in the goblets. Elinor handed it around. But she just walked over, picked up the tray, and carried it around. She had no chance to drug it.

"No, Mr. Forsythe, the only time the wine could have been drugged was when my brother was pouring it, when his body shielded the table from our eyes. When the police analyzed the dregs of the wine, every intact goblet showed traces of the drug. The goblet that Sebastian had broken still had enough wine on the shards to show no drug was in his goblet. And he had selected his own goblet, carried it away with him before the others were served."

"I had hoped, Miss Calvert, that you could give me some encouragement."

"I wish I could, but I can't very well lie, can I? There was too much evidence against Sebastian. He hadn't slept in his bed that night. He was still wearing the dinner jacket he'd worn the previous evening. The only one of us who was not drugged and helpless was my brother. I'm truly sorry. I would have liked to help. As far as Sebastian is concerned, proof of his innocence would accomplish nothing for him. Two people died that night, David and my brother. But for Elizabeth, for Rosemary and her sons, I wish I could change it."

Gently, Forsythe asked, "Have you seen your brother since—"

"Since they took him away? Yes, I went once. I hoped he might improve. The attendants tried to break through to him. They put pencils, crayons, paints on the table where he sat. He just sat there and stared. Then they tried modeling clay. He liked that. He picked only two colors, bright red and a grayish-blue. The day I was there, he sat there rolling it in his clumsy fingers." Forsythe had a fleeting thought of the hands that had fashioned the *Adonis*.

"Then I saw what he was doing. He was building a little figure, like children build snowmen, balls of clay piled one on the other. When he was finished, he lifted his hand, tightened it into a fist, and smashed the figure. The red and blue material oozed out between his fingers. His expression didn't change. Mine must have. His hands looked as they did that morning when Richard found him. I never went back. No, Mr. Forsythe, do what you wish, but in the end Elizabeth must accept the tragic fact that her father killed."

Forsythe quietly began to repack his case. "Nevertheless, it was good of you to trust me, to speak so frankly."

Melissa smiled slightly. "I phoned Sir Hilary. I haven't contacted him since the trial, but I still respect his opinion. He's the one who inspired the trust. He told me that you, despite the rumors I'd heard, deserved all the help I could give you. If anyone could uncover evidence to help my brother, he believes it will be you. Sir Hilary has a high opinion of your ability, says you have a devious mind, more suited to a detective than a barrister."

Forsythe rose. "He's very kind and so are you. I hope I deserve his faith and your confidences. Good day, Miss Calvert."

Melissa saw him out and then returned to her chair. She spread her hands on her lap. There was a tremor in the fingers. She stared down at them.

CHAPTER 9

Abigail Sanderson settled more comfortably against the leather seat. Turning the hood of the small car northward, Forsythe darted a glance at his companion.

"You're looking chipper today, Sandy. Are you looking forward to seeing Meads Green?"

"Partly. Mainly, I'm just glad to be out of that hotel suite. It was fine for you racing around meeting people, but it did get a bit tiresome for old faithful holding the fort with nothing but a tape recorder and typewriter for company."

"How did ex-Sergeant Hennessy strike you when you rang him up?"

"Exceedingly cordial, the hearty type. I could almost draw you a picture of him from his voice."

"Draw away."

"Over sixty, but of course we know that. Short, stocky, florid, and probably bald. I imagine a great floppy mustache. Polite but not the forelock-tugging kind."

Forsythe threw back his head and laughed. "Pretty difficult to tug a forelock with no hair."

"Come now, Robby; you know what I mean."

"I know what you're doing. Typing the poor chap. Your description fits every rural sergeant who ever appeared in novels or on telly."

"Very well, we'll make a bet. I'll give you five to one. One of your shillings to five of mine."

"With those odds I can't refuse. I don't mind taking your money at all."

They'd turned off the main road and were coasting down a gentle hill. Near the bottom, the car rumbled over a stone bridge and into a small village.

"There's the police station." Forsythe waved toward a green and white building.

"Keep going. The good sergeant lives on the next side street. Turn right, third house."

Obeying her instructions, Forsythe pulled up in front of a neat detached house. A box hedge surrounded it and the garden was a riot of color.

"Nice place to retire, Robby. Look, someone's coming now."

A tall man, lean and gray, strode down the walk toward them. With mirth in his eyes, Forsythe turned to his companion.

"Short, stocky, and florid, eh? Pay up."

Looking faintly downcast, Miss Sanderson climbed out of the car and waited for the man to open the gate. He no more than glanced at her as he brushed by and started briskly up the worn pavement. Another man was hurrying down the walk.

"Miss Sanderson, hello there; you're prompt. I suppose this is Mr. Forsythe. Do come in."

Forsythe shrugged his shoulders as his secretary threw a triumphant glance at him. Except that this man had a thick head of graying hair, her description fitted perfectly.

She managed to mutter in her employer's ear as they followed the stocky figure into the house, "Typecast, do I? You owe me."

"Come into the lounge. The wife's out; she'll be home soon. Imagine you'll want to talk to her too. I can make us some tea or perhaps a small spot of brandy?"

They followed him into a small, crowded room. He waited for them to be seated. Miss Sanderson smiled up at him and said expansively, "Brandy sounds like an excellent idea." Forsythe nodded, and their host poured three generous drinks.

"Now"—Hennessy sank into a shabby leather chair— "Sir Hilary Putham has been in touch, asked me to give you all the cooperation I can. Not that I wouldn't have anyway, seeing as how Mr. Sebastian's daughter is involved. I went over to the station and had a chat with the active sergeant. He was my constable when the murder was committed. We compared notes so's I wouldn't forget anything. Talked a bit to my wife about it too."

Miss Sanderson was looking perplexed. "You mentioned your wife before. Has she some connection with the case?"

"That she has. Meg—she was Meg Brady then—was helping at the Hall when this happened. We were thinking of marriage. I wanted her to chuck her job, but she wouldn't. Miss Melissa needed her, and Meg was fond of her. Meg became Mrs. Hennessy shortly after the trial."

"In that case," said Forsythe, "we certainly will want to talk with her."

"Where would you like me to start? The morning of the murder—"

"Before that, if you will. Did you or any of the people of the village have any idea of what was going on at the Hall?"

Hennessy nodded at Forsythe and settled more comfortably in his chair. "You mean Mr. Sebastian and the Mersey boy? No, we had no idea. Didn't know anything about it until after the murder. Couldn't believe it. Of course Mr. Sebastian never had anything to do with Meads Green. He was either at the Hall or in London. Same with his older brother, always away. When their father died, Miss Melissa took over. Good job she did too. Most of us have something to be grateful for. She saw nobody came to any harm. If money was scarce, she was always there—sickness, education for a lot of bright youngsters. Yes, she did well.

"After the trial when the newspapers and magazines sent their people around, the villagers wouldn't have anything to do with them. Figured it was none of their business. Can't say we liked what Mr. Sebastian had been up to, but he was a Calvert. Been a Calvert at the Hall as long as there's been a Meads Green. Not anymore, last one was Miss Melissa and she left in forty-four. Closed up the house and went to London. She still helps, though she hasn't much income now herself. Once in a while I let her know if someone's in real trouble and she scrapes up some money and sends it down for them."

Forsythe finished his brandy and set the glass to one side. "What did you think of the other people at the Hall?"

"Well, young Mersey came down to the village often. Nice young fellow, turned the girl's heads, you know; he was such a good-looking chap. But he was quiet, no airs. After Rosemary came home, she was here a lot too. Regular scamp, Rosemary, tomboyish as they come. We all liked her. Abby Temple kept as much stuff for her as she could, sweet buns and toffee, that sort of thing. The secretary, Horner, he came down to the stationers, picked up paper and books. Wild-eyed young man, he'd been badly stove up in North Africa. Pretty short and brusque, but he was a poet, you know."

Miss Sanderson's hand was flying over her shorthand pad. At this remark, she lifted her eyes and grinned at Forsythe.

Avoiding her eyes, he asked Hennessy, "When Miss Atlin and Mrs. Calvert arrived, were they in Meads Green at all?"

"Mrs. Calvert passed through a couple of times." His

mouth under the heavy mustache moved in a smile. "Every man, regardless of age, saw *her*. A lot different from the first Mrs. Calvert. Noticed her myself. Got in a little trouble with Meg about it. Too enthusiastic, I guess. Miss Atlin, she came down quite often too, with young Mersey and Rosemary. Picked up embroidery stuff and books from the lending library. Always stopped to pass the time with Clara Ben, she runs the bookstore. Seemed a decent enough person."

Hennessy struggled out of his chair and picked up the brandy bottle. "Little more for you?" Both his guests shook their heads and their host poured himself another drink. Forsythe waited until he was seated.

"Then there was nothing to lead up to the morning of the murder, no warning that all wasn't going well at the Hall?"

Hennessy shook his head. "Not a thing. Meg said that Miss Melissa was all nerves, didn't like Mrs. Calvert being there. But I had no idea what was going on. On the morning that Mersey was found dead, I got a call from Mr. Deveraux. It was early, at 6:46 A.M. Deveraux was pretty upset; I could tell that. He said Mersey was dead, murdered. Asked me to bring a doctor and come up fast as we could get there. I routed out my constable, Baines—we both slept in quarters behind the station—and I put in a call for Doctor Jarvis. He was an elderly man then. Been dead a good thirteen years. Doctor Jarvis said he'd meet us at the Hall.

"Baines and I went right up. Miss Melissa and Rosemary were upstairs. The rest of them were waiting in the drawing room. They'd partially closed the doors that led to the studio. Horner took us in, and there they both were. Baines had brought a camera, but he didn't take the pictures. He headed for the back door after one look. I could hear him outside." Hennessy slanted a look at Miss Sanderson. "It was bad, very bad, and Baines was just a young fellow. Never saw anything like it. I took a couple of shots of Mr. Sebastian and Mersey. Then Doctor Jarvis arrived.

"Mr. Sebastian was gone; his mind was finished. He just

sat there holding that thing, staring straight ahead. Well, we got him cleaned up and took him to the hospital. I knew I was out of my depth, the people involved and all. So I requested assistance from the Yard. I was glad to see them take over. Feeling as I did about the Calverts, it would have been rugged to have had to dig the truth out of poor Miss Melissa and the girl."

Forsythe eyed the other man. "You never had any reservations about Sebastian Calvert's guilt?"

Slowly, Hennessy's big head moved from side to side. "No doubt about it. He'd cracked up and did for the boy. I didn't like to believe it but . . ." He spread his hands.

"Your wife. How did she feel? She was closer to the people involved."

"Meg, well she—" Hennessy broke off and cocked his head. "Here she is now. She can tell you herself."

Hennessy had keen hearing. Both Forsythe and Miss Sanderson looked up. The woman who was entering the room was much younger than her husband. She was plump and neatly dressed, with a gentle, plain face.

Rising, her husband took her arm. "This is Miss Sanderson and Mr. Forsythe, my dear. They want to hear about the Hall and the people—"

She broke in, looking slightly flustered. "It was all so long ago, Henry. I don't know how I can help."

Her husband soothed her. "Just you sit down here, Meg. You do your best now; you know Mr. Sebastian's daughter is the one who wants to know how it was. We owe her that."

"Poor child. How dreadful it must be for her. How can I help, Mr. Forsythe?"

"Your husband said you didn't have any suspicion of what was going on between . . . any of the people at the Hall."

"That I didn't. I wouldn't have stayed on there even for Miss Melissa if I had. But Mr. Sebastian and Mr. Mersey, well, they didn't show anything. All I knew was that Mr. Mersey was posing for the statue. Never saw that either. I wasn't allowed in the studio. As for the rest of them, well, Miss Melissa was terribly put upon. She'd everything to do."

Miss Sanderson glanced up from her notebook. "It must have been awfully hard on you with such a small staff in a house the size of the Hall."

"Impossible. We did all we could. Old Hannah, the cook, did her best in the kitchen though she was poorly most of the time. Miss Melissa and me, we gave the first floor a lick and a promise. Kept the rooms as clean as we could. The bedrooms we never touched, or hardly ever. Miss Melissa laid it down; everyone must do their part. And some of them—you wouldn't believe it. After Miss Atlin come she helped us; took care of Mrs. Calvert's room as well as her own. More like a maid she was to that woman than a cousin, always fetching and carrying. I'd be upstairs once in a while, cleaning the hall or putting linen in the linen room, and I'd tidy up after Mr. Sebastian and Mr. Deveraux when he was down. Poor men, no idea even where to start."

"About Mrs. Calvert—" Forsythe began.

He'd touched a sore point. Mrs. Hennessy's gentle expression hardened. "Her! I've said it before and I'll say it again. Worthless trash, no better than a fancy trollop. Letting poor Miss Atlin wait on her hand and foot. Chasing after Mr. Mersey. No shame. Right in front of Miss Melissa and Rosemary."

"Now, now, Meg." Her husband leaned over and touched her hand.

She drew it away indignantly. "And you, Henry Hennessy, no better than the rest. Gawking at her when she come through the village."

Miss Sanderson's eyes were twinkling. Forsythe said softly, "Can you tell me about the last week, after Mr. Deveraux arrived?"

Mrs. Hennessy tore her eyes from her husband's face and looked at Forsythe. "I wasn't there. Left the Friday night before Mr. Deveraux come. My sister, she was having her first child, and Miss Melissa said to go to her. Said things couldn't get in a worse mess than they already was. Afterward I was glad I went. It was a horrible thing."

They were all silent for a moment. Then Mrs. Hennessy added, "I'm sorry. I'd like to help Mr. Sebastian's girl. It's just that there's nothing I can say."

Forsythe rose. "You've tried. That's the main thing; you've tried." He looked at her husband. "Do you suppose we could go up and have a look at the Hall?"

The older man pulled himself out of the depths of the leather chair. "You certainly can. I'll get the keys and take you right up."

"Henry."

Hennessy paused at the sound of his wife's voice.

"Have you forgotten the christening party?" She looked apologetically at Forsythe. "Our grandson, we have three now, the latest one is being christened today. He's named after my husband. Our daughter will be heartbroken if we don't come."

Hennessy looked at her with a harassed expression. "That's right. I'd clean forgotten."

"Perhaps Miss Sanderson and I can go up alone," Forsythe offered. "That is, if you think it would be all right."

Hennessy beamed with relief. "Certainly. Sorry, but that's how it is with a family. I'll get the keys."

Snapping her notebook closed, Miss Sanderson returned her pen to her handbag. She looked up at Mrs. Hennessy. "Has the Hall been unoccupied all these years?"

"Never been a soul living in it. Miss Melissa just locked it up and gave Henry the keys. We look after it as best we can. Henry gets a couple of the lads and chops at the grounds once in a while. I do my best inside. We keep some heat going in the winter." She sighed. "Seems a terrible shame. Such a place, and a happy home it once was."

"No trouble with vandalism?" asked Forsythe.

"The villagers would never go near it. As for the day trippers and the reporters," her lips curled slightly, "Henry soon sets them right. All the looking they do is though the bars on the gates and they can hardly see the house from there."

Henry had returned. He handed Forsythe a ring of keys. "They're labeled. You won't have any trouble finding the place. Go along to the end of the main street, turn right on White Rose Lane, and keep going. It's near the top of the hill. Big iron gates. Are you planning to stay over tonight?"

Forsythe nodded. "It will be a little late to start back to London."

"I thought you might. I spread the word. There'll be rooms for you at the Inn. Stan and Bea will see you're comfortable." He noticed Miss Sanderson's baffled look. "The villagers don't take well to strangers, specially ones wondering about the Calverts and the Hall. But they know who you are and who you're working for and they don't mind that."

Forsythe nodded his appreciation. "Fine. Thank you, Sergeant Hennessy and Mrs. Hennessy. We'll get the keys back to you."

Beside their car, Miss Sanderson paused. "How about walking, Robby? After a week vegetating, I can use the exercise."

"Good idea." He took her arm. "We can work up an appetite for Bea's tea. With our sergeant recommending us, I have a hunch it may be formidable."

White Rose Lane had only a few scattered cottages along it. They were set back from the lane and looked drowsy and peaceful. They'd seen only one person, a very old man, dozing under the shade of a plane tree. The scents from the gardens floated to them, spicy and sweet, carnations and roses. Somewhere in the distance a dog rattled its chain and barked.

Beyond the last cottage, the road wound upward, steadily but gently. Partway up, Miss Sanderson laid a hand on her companion's arm. They stopped and looked back at the valley and the village streets.

"Looks a haven of peace, doesn't it? Impossible to believe, looking at it, that violence ever happened here."

Forsythe leaned against a wooden stile set into a low stone wall. "People create the violence, Sandy, not the place. In even the most civilized of us is still that seed of violence. It requires only the right set of circumstances to bring it out."

Climbing onto the stile, Miss Sanderson sat down. She plucked a long tuft of grass and nibbled on it. "Even in thou and I, old philosopher." She gazed thoughtfully down on Meads Green. "Speaking of violence, you don't seem to be overly disturbed about someone taking a shot at you."

"As you may have noticed, I haven't been taking any chances. I've been rather careful where I go and how."

"You also had an eye on the rearview mirror all the way from London. Expecting company?"

"Just checking, that's all."

She cast a glance at his profile. "I have noticed one thing. For the last couple of days, you've had the same smug look around the mouth that I've learned to recognize. Your father had that expression when he'd found a hole in the prosecution's case and was getting set to blow it to bits. I've plowed through the same stuff you have and I can't see a ray of light. Like to share what you're thinking?"

"There's a pattern emerging. I even thought for a short time that I could name the murderer. But there's something wrong with my theory, something that still doesn't fit. Haven't you any idea yet?"

"Scads. That's what's wrong, just too damn many. The Freudian slips in those tapes have me grasping at one person, then another. Take Melissa, for instance. One minute she announces she doesn't even dislike Vanessa. The next minute she gets all worked up and states she can't understand why Vanessa wasn't killed instead of Mersey. Confusing. But the original evidence against Sebastian—as far as I can see—it still stands."

Forsythe held out his hand to her. "Jump down, old girl; you've rested long enough. I can see the gates that the sergeant mentioned from here." They started up the hill. "You're mistaken, Sandy; the evidence against Calvert has holes all through it. But enough of surmising. As they say in the shilling shockers, let's get on to the scene of the crime."

Forsythe ignored the huge iron gates. Selecting a key, he opened a small grilled door set to one side. As soon as they were though it, he carefully relocked it. The remains of a gardener's cottage stood beside the gate. Then the driveway twisted away between huge oaks toward a corner of a house. They could see it more clearly as they turned the first curve.

Miss Sanderson was looking critically at the grounds. "Blimey, it's been a while since Hennessy and his lads have been up here chopping. Look at the undergrowth."

"Forget the grounds and have a look at the house. Smasher, isn't it?"

"Perfectly lovely."

It was. The long sprawling building had graceful proportions. Even the neglect in its surroundings couldn't detract from the lines. Wooden shutters were closed over the upper windows, but the lower ones were uncovered. The front door was hand-carved and had an ancient knocker shaped in the form of a dragon. Forsythe checked the key ring and opened the door.

Standing on the green and white tile of the foyer, Miss Sanderson gazed up the long sweeping flight of stairs. "Where do we start?"

His eyes followed hers. "Might as well go straight up. Just a minute. I have the floor plan." He stopped two-thirds of the way up. "You go on, Sandy; Mersey's room was the first on the right. Open the door, stand in front of it for a minute, and then saunter down the hall."

She obeyed. Forsythe stood where he was, his eyes on her.

"I'm right down at the end, where the hall branches toward the servant's wing. Is that far enough?"

"Fine." He climbed the rest of the stairs and walked down the hall toward her. It was dim and the air was stale. "Let's check the room Deveraux used. It's two rooms down from Mersey's."

She rejoined him. The room was quite dark, heavy furniture looming out from the walls. Forsythe threw up the window sash and unbolted the shutters. He heard his secretary's sigh of satisfaction as the sun came streaming in.

"Ruddy mausoleum," she muttered as she stepped up beside him.

They both leaned over the sill, their eyes sweeping the area directly below them. Forsythe leaned out further. "There's the terrace and the steps leading down."

"The garden must have been beautiful when this happened, Robby. It's a tangle now, but you can still see traces. Look at the roses. What a sight they must have been when they were properly tended."

He pulled the shutters closed and bolted them. "Let's have a look at the lower floor."

At the foot of the stairs, Miss Sanderson started to turn left. Forsythe touched her arm.

"This side first. Let me see." He swung open the first door. "Sebastian's study, nothing for us there."

"Mrs. Hennessy hasn't done badly, Robby. Lots of dust, but no signs of cobwebs, and the furniture is carefully covered. All the pictures and ornaments are gone. Melissa must have either sold them or had them stored."

Forsythe opened the second door. "Probably sold them. She needs the money. I'm surprised she hasn't sold the whole property. Ah, the dining room, and beyond, the terrace. Let's have a closer look at that garden you were admiring."

He opened the French door and they stepped out. For-sythe leaned against one of the stone pillars at the edge of the terrace. The rough surface was warm under his hand. His companion wandered down the shallow steps into the garden. Picking her way through the tangled growth, she headed toward a clump of rosebushes. Selecting a large yellow bloom, she pinned it carefully to her jacket. Forsythe wasn't watching her. He appeared to be gazing into space.

She retraced her steps. "Damn shame, letting a beautiful place like this stand empty." She looked sharply up at Forsythe. "Hey, wake up. What are you thinking about?"

He started. "Nothing, Sandy. Come along; we'll have a quick look at the other side of the house."

The drawing room opened directly off the foyer. It was an enormous room. Rose velvet covered long, mullioned windows. Miss Sanderson drew them back from the front window. She stood with her back to it, gazing around.

"Look at the way the colors have been blended, Robby. Whoever decorated this room had taste. Everything perfectly coordinated. These drapes are finished; the velvet's rotted clear through. But look at their color against the deeper rose of the rug. And the furniture," she pulled a dust cover off the chair nearest her, "ah, just as I hoped, rose brocade picked out with the same ivory as the walls." She bent closer and inspected the arm of the chair. "The brocade's rotted too. How could anyone let this happen?"

Forsythe was walking toward the double doors at the other end of the room. "I suppose Melissa just couldn't stand it. She loved this place, everything it stood for. Her dreams turned into a nightmare, and she's letting the house crumble away."

He swung the doors wide. Joining him, Miss Sanderson looked into the studio. It was as large as the drawing room. It was empty. Two walls were paned with glass and the floor was worn stone tile. The sun was streaming across the room. It should have been warm. It wasn't. She shivered and moved closer to her companion. He was looking with interest at the inside wall. Dust-coated daggers and medieval swords were arranged down its length.

"That's where the scimitar must have hung."

Miss Sanderson followed his eyes and then turned back to the drawing room. She slipped and nearly fell. Moving quickly, Forsythe steadied her.

"Take it easy, Sandy. There's moss growing on the stones in places. You could break your neck."

They both looked down at the gray-green fungus clinging damply to the stone.

"Let's get out of here, Robby." She pulled her arm from his grasp and walked swiftly across the rose-colored rug toward the foyer.

"What's the matter with you?" Forsythe called after her. "Wait for just a minute. I want to check the lock on the French door in the dining room."

His secretary paused by the front door. One hand brushed at the neck of her sweater. Her sleeve caught the yellow rose. Slowly, several petals drifted to the floor.

"Check away. I'll wait for you outside."

When he came out a few minutes later, Forsythe found her standing in the middle of the driveway. She was staring up at the gray stone bulk of the Hall. Her face was grave, almost cold.

Forsythe grinned. "What spooked you, my intrepid friend? One minute you're going on about how lovely the house is; the next you take off like a scalded cat."

She didn't smile back. Forsythe looked more closely at her. Then he took her arm and turned her away from the house, toward the gates. The old trees closed off the sun. They moved through shadows.

When Miss Sanderson spoke, her voice was muffled. Forsythe had to strain to hear her.

"Don't laugh, Robby. Do you believe in ghosts?"

"I certainly don't and neither do you."

"Well, do you believe that sometimes houses have auras, that you can sense something waiting?"

He squeezed her arm. "No to that, too."

She looked directly into his eyes. "I don't like this place. I'll be glad to get out of it." She hastened her step. They were nearing the gates.

"Look, Sandy, you're not a fanciful woman. Be sensible. You knew the history of that house. You were fine until you stepped into the studio, the spot you've heard so much about. Then your imagination took over. Houses don't have auras. People's minds supply them."

Her pale eyes were wide. "I could almost see someone pulling a cover over Deveraux, then stepping into that damn stone-floored room and lifting a scimitar over David's body. But there's no sense in trying to explain to you. At times you're revoltingly logical." She tried for a grin. "You're also probably right. Let's get back to Meads Green and have tea. On second thought, I may skip the tea and have something stronger. Anyway, I'll be glad to get back to London tomorrow."

Forsythe closed the grilled door behind them and re-locked it. Without looking at her he said, "We won't be going back to London tomorrow."

She waited for him to turn to face her. "Just what will we be doing?"

"No matter how you feel about the Hall, we'll have to go back to it one more time. That's where it started. It seems a fitting place for it to end. I want you to get in touch with the five people connected with this case. Wire Vanessa in Rome, and let them know we're having a get-together party."

Her voice was level. "When and why?"

He pulled out his pipe and tobacco pouch. "In three days, it will be the twenty-fifth of August, exactly twenty-five years since the death of Adonis. You may have seen ghosts at the Hall. I saw the face of a murderer. A quarter of a century is a long time to go blameless while another man has to take the guilt. It's time the killer was unmasked. Elizabeth is most impatient. Ring her first."

"Do you think all of them will consent to come? We can't force them, you know."

"They have no choice," he said grimly. "They've all tried to show Sebastian either guilty as hell or innocent. If one of them is afraid to turn up now, what would that prove?"

Miss Sanderson was tapping her nail against her front tooth. It was the only sound on the quiet road. After a moment, she dropped her hand to her lapel. The remains of the rose she unpinned and held in her hand. They both stared down at it.

She said quietly. "The only one who would fear this meeting is the murderer. You're right; they'll all be here." Her fingers loosened and the rose fell to the road. "Including our killer."

CHAPTER 10

The rose-shaded lamplight and the flickering glow from the fireplace were kind to the room. They disguised the rents in the velvet hangings, the tears in the rich brocade, the worn spots on the rug. The drawing room of Calvert Hall looked as it must have twenty-five years earlier. The furniture was uncovered, ashtrays now dotted the low tables, and on a chest at the end of the room an assortment of glasses and bottles were arrayed.

Forsythe stood with his back to the fire, his feet slightly apart, his hands clasped behind him. His face was relaxed, any tension within him was carefully concealed. At the left of the fireplace, on a long table that years before had held a tray of wine goblets, Sandy had set herself up. In front of her were neatly arranged a tape recorder, a pile of boxed tapes, and a number of cardboard folders. At the end of the table, ex-Sergeant Hennessy relaxed in the room's largest chair.

Forsythe looked at the rest of the gathering. The chairs in which they were seated were arranged in a semicircle around him, each chair placed a good distance from the next. All but one of the witnesses from the trial of Sebastian Calvert were present.

To his right was Elizabeth Calvert Pennell, clad in a dark suit that blended with the shadowed corner she had selected. Her eyes were flicking from face to face, settling on none but seeing all. Near her, Melissa Calvert sat, her feet close together, her thin shoulders erect. Richard Deveraux was beside his friend's sister. He wasn't watching Forsythe. His eyes ranged past Rosemary Horner, who sat on his other side, to Vanessa Calvert. Vanessa was very much at her ease. The soft lighting was as kind to her as it was to the room. She wore a high-necked amber gown and a tiny matching hat clinging precariously to her red curls. Against the back of her chair was tossed a honey mink stole. The last member of the group, John Horner, was seated between Vanessa and Sandy's table. His eyes were hard on Forsythe and had been since he'd entered the room.

Horner spoke now, a forced lightness in his voice. "This looks much like the setting of one of my early novels. All the suspects seated with their faces in a good light. The famous detective, or in this case barrister, facing them. The stolid policeman quietly waiting to make the arrest." He jerked his head toward Hennessy.

"Ex-policeman, sir, and not here in an offical capacity. Mr. Forsythe was kind enough to invite me to sit in simply because I was here at the beginning."

Forsythe smiled at Horner. "That's correct. We're all here for a purpose. I'm here to disprove the charges against Sebastian Calvert and you're here for your own private reasons. For a time, I may sound more like a teacher than a detective, but bear with me—and I'd appreciate it if none of you interrupt. There'll be time to question later.

"Elizabeth Pennell, as you are all aware, came to me for help. I began to check the old case out, not with any real hopes

for success, but I determined to treat it as I would a case I was
defending in court. Sebastian is my client. To prove him innocent, I had to suspect each of you in turn.

"I soon found a sound basis to support Sebastian's innocence. David Mersey was not the perfect physical specimen he
appeared to be. Like many of us, he had a weakness. He was
a diabetic. Sebastian, if he had been capable of organizing Mersey's death in the way he was accused of, would have been
capable of killing him simply by using this weakness for his own
means.

"There was also Sebastian's temperament to take into
account. Sebastian was far from a strong person. He'd allowed
his sister to push him into his first marriage. He was shattered
by his second and came home to let his relatives and friends
pick up the pieces for him.

"Are we to believe that Sebastian would deliberately and
for the first time make a decisive move and kill Mersey? Then
there was his attachment to the boy. After two disastrous mar-
riages, he turned his back on the female sex and chose this boy
as his love object. When Mersey decided to leave him, it would
have been more in Sebastian's character to go to pieces again,
but not to kill Mersey and butcher the body he worshipped.

"So I took the opposite tack. If Sebastian Calvert was
innocent, he was not the one who had drugged a house full of
people. He was drugged as they were. Only the murderer was
conscious that night."

"But the wine. I told you my brother—" Melissa suddenly covered her mouth with her hand. "I'm sorry, you asked
us not to interrupt."

Forsythe looked at her. "The wine is going to have to
be overlooked at this point. Later, in its proper place, I will
prove that your brother did not drug the wine."

His eyes left Melissa's face and swung around the circle
of faces. "To continue. I proceeded to do the thing the police
should have done at the time of the murder—look for motives.

I didn't have to look far. As my right-hand girl, Miss Sanderson, will tell you, there was an embarrassment of motives."

"Motives?" This was Horner. "What motive could any of us have had?"

"Let's take you first, Horner. What was the general situation in forty-four? Not just at Calvert Hall, but all over England."

Horner looked puzzled. "It was wartime, the fifth year of a bloody horrible war."

"Exactly, a bloody horrible war. All of you had lived through the Blitz. Violence had become commonplace. Each of you was a strong, able person. Who did we have thrown together under this roof? A man who would later be a famous writer; an equally famous publisher; a decisive woman who not only ruled her own family but an entire estate; a brilliant and precocious girl; a woman who laid down her life in a daring rescue; and Vanessa. I don't think we'll argue about Vanessa. You all recognize her qualities.

"All of these people had personal problems of their own. Then they're thrown together in a set of circumstances that erupts into murder."

Horner had been lighting a cigarette. He gazed through the smoke at Forsythe. "Very well, barrister, the background was hardly normal. I'll give you that. Present your case against the famous writer."

"It's obvious, Horner. In your own words you were unstable, had a nasty case of war nerves. You certainly were no stranger to killing. You were straight from the battlefields of North Africa. Into your life comes Vanessa. Not only do you want her, you want her with every fiber of your being. Vanessa not only preferred Mersey to you, but humilates you about your size. Little Jack Horner was quite capable of venting his rage against the big handsome man she wanted. Killing Mersey would be double-bladed revenge. Vanessa would be hurt badly."

Horner squinted through the cloud of gray smoke. "Not bad, Forsythe, proceed."

"Melissa is next. I don't have to outline her qualifications. You know her. Her obsession really was her brother's work. She was prepared to do anything for it. She managed Sebastian, drove him, forced him into a loveless marriage, and accepted a homosexual relationship in her own beloved home to further his career. Melissa is a woman of rigid morals apart from her brother. Think of the shattering effect on her when she learned her sacrifices were in vain. At the apex of his career, her brother was, as she said to Richard Deveraux, 'finally ruined by David and Vanessa.' By killing David, Melissa would also have her revenge on both of them."

Richard Deveraux interrupted. "You're wrong there, Forsythe. Perhaps Melissa did have a motive, but do you actually think anyone her size could carry a big man like Mersey down a flight of stairs to the studio?"

Forsythe shifted slightly. "This point, like the drugging of the wine, will have to wait. We aren't yet discussing the means, only the motives. Let's look at our next candidate for murderer. Elinor Atlin, the colorless one, the woman who always faded into the background—"

Vanessa spoke. It was the first time she had broken her silence. "Can't we leave Lin out of this? She's dead—"

"She was very much alive at the time of the murder. Here we have a repressed woman, devoted to her cousin, and capable of fast thinking and action. Her death proves that. Also possessed of enormous physical strength. Both Vanessa and Elinor were large women. Elinor was an athlete, able to handle Vanessa when Deveraux and Horner couldn't. Elinor depended on Vanessa financially as well as in every other way. She'd already been, in her own words, "deserted by Vanessa" during her brief marriage to Sebastian. She did her best to talk Mersey out of this alliance. Elinor could have killed the boy to keep him away from Vanessa."

"That sounds pretty weak," Horner commented.

"Murders have been committed for weaker motives than that," Forsythe answered. He glanced down. Miss Sanderson was vigorously tugging at his jacket. "What do you want, Sandy?"

"But—"

"Are you going to start interrupting, too?" Forsythe asked good naturedly. She subsided in injured silence, and her employer continued. "We come to our fourth suspect—Richard Deveraux. Here we have a mature man, admired by women, but not captivated by any one of them. He finally meets the woman he always has wanted, Vanessa, his best friend's estranged wife. How strong his devotion is we can see before us. Deveraux claims his obesity is the result of compensation. He prefers to believe that it is guilt for Sebastian's crime that drives him toward the gluttony that slowly is killing him. Deveraux is deluding himself. I believe he accepted that guilt long since. He never accepted Vanessa's loss. He not only lost her, but saw her in a love scene with David. A man of Richard's caliber could quite easily plan and execute the crime. Again with two objectives, the destruction of a hated rival and the injury of Vanessa."

Vanessa stretched and smiled. "Wonderful! So far everyone wants to kill because they because they either adore me or hate my intestines. I had no idea I could inspire such feelings."

"I think you're being truthful, Mrs. Calvert," Forsythe said dryly. "Melissa's description of you is apt. You really are a poltergeist."

Her amber eyes widened. "A *what?*"

"Never mind. Let us go on. Number five—Rosemary Calvert Horner."

"Mr. Forsythe." It was Melissa. "My niece was a child at the time. I'd prefer we kept her out of this."

"As you would have preferred they'd kept her out of the actual trial? It can't be done. Rosemary also had a motive. You call her a child. She was not a child. She was a big, adolescent girl, strong and highly intelligent. Rosemary was capable of violence. Her attack on a teacher proves this. Furthermore, she idolized her uncle. Rosemary felt she'd almost lost him when he returned from Ireland. Here was the same woman, Vanessa, threatening him again. In the girl's eyes, David was a traitor, as guilty as Vanessa. It occurs to me that Rosemary might have killed Mersey."

Horner grunted. "I don't know about the rest of you, but I could use a drink."

Forsythe turned to his secretary. "Would you do the honors, Sandy?"

While she was fixing the drinks, they sat silently. They accepted their glasses just as silently and waited for Forsythe to continue.

"There are serious flaws in my reasoning. We'll take the one Deveraux mentioned. Melissa could have done the first part of the crime, the actual murder by morphine. So could Rosemary. She'd worked in the hospital and either given injections or seen hypodermic needles used. Rosemary was large for her age, but neither Melissa nor she had the strength to carry Mersey that far. The rest of the suspects, Elinor, Deveraux, Horner, could have done both parts. But there was the problem of Sebastian. To be innocent, he had to be drugged and helpless. How did he get down to the studio?"

"For a time I thought I had the answer. Deveraux had slept the night through in the drawing room, fully clothed. What if Sebastian hadn't been able to undress before the drug hit him? He might have collapsed on his bed. Drugs affect different people different ways. Very well, I tried picturing Sebastian waking first, going to David's room. The boy is on his bed, dead, the hypodermic needle and the case beside him. There would be only one reason for Sebastian to complete the pattern, carry the body downstairs, and disfigure it—an effort to divert suspicion from someone Sebastian cared for. For his sister or niece, a man, even one as weak as Sebastion, might have tried to cover up."

Horner leaned forward, his hands clenched on his knees, his jaw jutting. "Just one minute. Why couldn't Calvert have passed out fully dressed and instead of going to David's room when he came to, come directly down to the studio? He could have found the mutilated body, gathered it up in his arms, and gone quietly insane. That fits just as well."

"I agree, Horner; I considered that theory also. But there's one flaw that shoots holes in both those ideas. My mental efforts to get Sebastian fully dressed into the studio with the murdered man—well, I'll show you. Sandy, got the tapes ready?"

She nodded and pressed the button. They heard Horner's voice. ". . . the members of the household and guests must tidy their own rooms. The women were fine at this and I looked after mine army style. But you should have seen Sebastian's and Richard's. I don't think they ever did more than pull the bedspreads over their crumpled sheets and blankets."

Miss Sanderson depressed the switch and Horner's voice stopped abruptly.

Horner moved impatiently. "Okay, so Sebastian was a messy bedmaker, what in—"

Forsythe raised his hand. "The next tape is Deveraux's. He's telling me about the morning of the murder, just before Sebastian was taken away. Sandy."

She arranged another tape and Deveraux's rich baritone echoed through the room. "I sat down on his bed and broke right up. Gradually I pulled myself together, got up, and started automatically to straighten the bedspread again. Funny the things we do under stress. There—"

Horner still looked baffled, but sick comprehension was looking from Richard Deveraux's eyes. Forsythe asked the big man, "Why did you say 'again'?"

"I'd rumpled it where I sat. And the bed was neat, the

spread pulled tautly over it, perfectly made." Deveraux rubbed one hand across his eyes. "All these years," he muttered, "it was right in front of me and I never saw it. Sebastian never made that bed. Someone else did."

Forsythe repeated slowly. "Sebastian never made the bed. The only other person who ever touched his room was Meg Brady, and she was away that week. Now we know that Sebastian went to bed that night and slept the same way the rest of you did, a deeply drugged sleep. Deep enough for the murderer to dress him in his dinner jacket, carry him downstairs, and leave him in the studio with the corpse of David Mersey in his arms. Then the killer went up and methodically made up Sebastian's bed. The killer slipped there by making it neatly. But in the state the rest of you were in afterward, nobody noticed it. When Sebastian roused from his drugged slumber that morning, think what he saw, what he held in his arms. Does anyone wonder that his mind gave?"

"Why?" It was only a whisper from Melissa's pale lips.

"Because," said Forsythe, "this was a crime of passion. The passion was hate. You said yourself, Miss Calvert, that two men died that night. I don't think the murderer counted on Sebastian losing his mind, but it served just as well. The idea was that Sebastian would be accused of the crime, be tried, and executed. We can see that Sebastian was supposed to suffer more than David Mersey. This explains why David was killed painlessly with morphine before the scimitar was used. The murderer couldn't bear to cut into his living body."

Forsythe paused and looked at Horner. "You were right about the malevolence in the drawing room that night, but it didn't emanate from Sebastian. It came from another mind, cooly waiting for the drug to take effect to cover the sounds of two heavy bodies, one unconscious, the other dead, being carried down the stairs."

Rosemary shuddered. Her taffy hair was bright against the pallor of her face. "Who could hate that much?"

Horner looked at his wife. Then he rose and stood behind her chair, his hands gripping her shoulders.

Forsythe continued. "I lost all my suspects at one fell go. Rosemary, Melissa, Deveraux would never deliberately implicate Sebastian. Horner didn't like his employer, but he respected him as an artist and was grateful for his help. Elinor Atlin might kill to keep her cousin, but she most certainly wouldn't have any reason to pull Sebastian in on it."

Vanessa touched her lighter to a cigarette. "I could have shot that theory down when you outlined it. Lin didn't stay with me after the trial. If she'd thought enough of me to kill, she certainly wouldn't have left me and gone to Switzerland."

"That's what I was trying to say, Robby, when I was pulling at your jacket," observed Miss Sanderson.

Horner spoke from behind his wife's chair. "You've talked yourself out of suspects, Forsythe."

"Not quite. There's still one left." Forsythe's hands fell from behind his back. They were clenched into fists. He looked directly at the woman on the chair next to Rosemary. Her head was tilted back and her eyes were narrowed through the smoke of her cigarette.

"What about Vanessa Calvert?"

CHAPTER 11

Vanessa leaned over and butted her cigarette. She smiled brilliantly at Forsythe. "Hurrah! What *about* Vanessa Calvert? Now I don't feel so left out."

"You were never left out," Forsythe said grimly. "When I realized hate, directed mainly toward Sebastian, was the motive, you were the one I concentrated on."

Horner broke in. "You know you almost had me hypnotized for a while. Figured you should be the writer, not me. But your plot failed. I'm only too willing to pin this on Vanessa and I'll agree that the way she felt about her husband might have inspired part of the crime. But my mind boggles at the thought of Vanessa sacrificing a boy she was infatuated with and wanted to take with her just for the fun of seeing her husband executed. Vanessa is too much of a connoisseur of male flesh for that. Of all of us she was the only one with nothing to gain from David's death."

Forsythe hadn't moved his eyes from Vanessa's face.

"What they don't realize, Vanessa, is that Mersey never had any intention of leaving Sebastian. He wasn't going anywhere with you, was he?"

Everyone was talking at once. Forsythe held up his hand and their voices stilled one by one.

"You were all there; you kept saying it. But you couldn't see what was happening the day of the twenty-fifth. Just what proof did you have that David, in his showdown with Sebastian, had actually decided to throw in his lot with Vanessa?"

Deveraux spoke. "Elinor's testimony at the trial, and Rosemary overheard the conversation by the lake."

Forsythe turned to Miss Sanderson. "Give us the gist of Elinor Atlin's testimony, not word for word."

Flipping open a folder, Miss Sanderson started to speak, her voice dry and precise. "Elinor Atlin testified under oath that she approached David Mersey on the morning of August twenty-fifth, 1944. Mersey had just spoken with Sebastian Calvert. David Mersey told her that Calvert had tried to persuade him to give up his estranged wife. Calvert pointed out to Mersey the many advantages he would have if he stayed on at the Hall. Mersey felt that Vanessa Calvert was also wealthy and could give him the same things. Miss Atlin said she tried to tell the boy what Vanessa was like, that she would drop him like a toy when she tired of him. She asked Mersey whether his decision was definite. He answered it was. Then she asked whether Mersey had told Calvert of his decision. He again answered yes. She told him he would be ruining his life. Then—"

"That will do, Sandy." Forsythe swung back to the rest. "From there on Rosemary was listening. She didn't hear the entire conversation, only the end of it. And even that part was not all audible. In Rosemary's testimony there is no real evidence of *whom* David had chosen. Think back carefully."

Rosemary moved restlessly. "But that one sentence. I heard it clearly. Elinor knew that Vanessa would leave her again. She said—"

"We'll get to that sentence. Let's consider this. If David Mersey told Elinor that he intended to remain with Sebastian, do you think she would have betrayed her cousin? Would Elinor have given testimony that would have given *Vanessa* the only motive to kill the boy? Elinor could no longer help Sebastian. He was hopelessly insane.

"Now think back to what happened directly after the meeting at the lake. David did not seek out Vanessa. She was on the terrace. He came in the front door, went straight up to his room, and remained there. Does that sound like a young man so madly in love that he had just renounced Sebastian and the security he offered? No. All any of you had to go on was Elinor's story and the little that Rosemary heard that seemed to bear it out.

"Now we come to dinner, the only time that day you were together. Here we have Sebastian Calvert, a man who crumbles under hurt. Yet at dinner, you say he's almost manic, talkative, his eyes bright, his color high—not crushed but exhilarated. You didn't see a man who had lost. You saw a man who not only had finished his greatest work, the *Adonis*, but also received Mersey's word that he would remain with him."

"You're right," Horner muttered, "by God, you're right. Then Vanessa drugged the wine. I have no idea how, but I think you can explain that. She waited until we were all unconscious and proceeded to kill Mersey and arrange the scene. Think of it, the two men who had rejected her destroyed at one go."

Everyone but Deveraux nodded their heads. They were silent. It was a stony, frightening silence. Vanessa looked only at Deveraux. Her mouth was suddenly younger, more vulnerable.

"I know you have no reason to believe me. But I swear to you that I never killed anyone. I didn't." Her eyes dropped away from whatever she read in the man's face.

Forsythe moved from the hearth to Vanessa's side. He

stood there, one hand hovering over her shoulder. Slowly he moved it and rested it on the back of her chair.

"I know you didn't *kill*, Vanessa. But you are guilty, guilty of protecting the murderer all these years. To do it, you've taken the scorn from these people and the world."

Horner left his wife to face Forsythe. "Are you mad?"

Forsythe waved him back. "Totally sane. Vanessa was the one I believed guilty until the other day in this room. Sandy said something and the whole thing fell into place. All the bits and pieces that wouldn't fit were complete."

Miss Sanderson was staring at him, her mouth slightly open. "I said something? Do you mean in the studio?"

"I mean right here."

His secretary looked around the drawing room. "All I said in here was that I admired the way the colors had been blended. The various shades of rose so beautifully coordinated."

"That's all you said, Sandy. Then I heard Melissa's voice again. I heard her say three little words, vital words, and I knew that Vanessa couldn't be the killer. She had no reason to kill Mersey."

He looked around the intent circle of faces. "We've ignored the one person who was most important—David Mersey. Who was David Mersey? All your memories told me that he was an ordinary young man with an extraordinary amount of good looks. Aside from his beauty, he was good-natured, not bright, a chameleon who was able to ape manners and speech. But was he capable of dissembling the way he seemed to?

"Mersey's outward reaction to Vanessa was dislike and embarrassment. He avoided her. He avoided her because he *really* didn't like her; she repulsed him. All any of you could see was Vanessa. You couldn't see the forest for the trees. Just who did Mersey spend his time with besides young Rosemary? Who did he swim, play tennis, go to the village with? Who sought him out to learn his decision about Sebastian?"

Melissa looked at him, understanding flashing across her face. "Elinor Atlin."

"Elinor Atlin, the colorless one. David worshipped his mother. You've called her a patient Griselda, drab, a saint. Who fits that description better than Elinor?"

"Wait a minute." Rosemary was leaning forward, her gray eyes wide. "I saw Vanessa coming out of David's room. So did my aunt."

"And I," echoed Deveraux, "saw them in the garden. Or are you going to say that some other man was holding Vanessa?"

Forsythe nodded. "It was David. But the woman in his arms was not Vanessa." He moved slightly. "You, Deveraux, had a quick look at the scene below in moonlight. Rosemary only had a glimpse of a tall woman in a long negligee walking down a dimly lit hall. She mentioned long reddish hair. Elinor was built much like her cousin; her hair was gingery; she wore it long, 'strained back in a bun.' The woman you both saw was Elinor Atlin. The only person who had a close look at her was Melissa."

Melissa's fingers were pleating the silk of her skirt. "Are you saying I lied, Mr. Forsythe?"

"No, I say you told the truth about what you *thought* you saw. If I remember correctly, Rosemary had broken your glasses the previous week. You needed those glasses. I checked and found that it would not be likely you'd have them back the following Wednesday. They had to be sent from London."

Melissa was staring at him. "I didn't have them. And I closed my eyes. I didn't see which room Vanessa, or the woman I was positive was Vanessa, went into. But when I went to Vanessa's room a few minutes after—"

"How long after?" Forsythe broke in.

"Not long. I put Rosemary to bed, perhaps ten minutes."

"Ten minutes later you found Vanessa in bed, reading

a novel and eating chocolates—strange behavior for a passionate woman who was supposed to have just come from her lover's embrace. But that wasn't all. Vanessa was wrapped in a blanket. You said the upper part of her body was covered by it. You couldn't see the color of her nightgown, but she wore in her hair—these are the three vital words—a *green satin ribbon.*"

He paused and gestured toward the woman sitting quietly beside Rosemary. "Look at Vanessa. What is she wearing, Rosemary?"

"Why, a golden or amber dress, matching hat, shoes, and bag."

Forsythe touched the mink stole. "Even her fur is honey-colored. Color-coordinated, that is Vanessa's trademark. The morning of her arrival at the Hall, we have Vanessa all in white. Rosemary sees her wardrobe. Shoes, dresses, hats, all in matching colors. The night Horner went to Vanessa's room to plead his case, what was she wearing?—a purple gown and headband.

"Can you imagine a woman so sensitive to color going to meet her lover wearing a green ribbon in her hair and," he turned to Rosemary, "what color was the woman who came out of David's room wearing?"

"Pale blue."

"You've hit it, by God." Horner was excited. "But why would Vanessa let Melissa believe it was her that night?"

"Right in character for her, Horner. No one has ever accused Vanessa of being a small person. She knew at once it had to be her cousin, her *quiet* cousin, having an affair with Mersey. Vanessa was amused. She loves mischief. If she couldn't get to David, very well, let Elinor have him. Vanessa covered for Elinor gladly and diverted your attention from the lovers.

"Vanessa let Sebastian think the same thing. She enjoyed every moment of their meeting in the garden. She knew

Sebastian would find out the truth from David, but in the meantime she was having a wonderful time baiting her husband.

"David did tell Sebastian, but they must have struck a gentleman's agreement. David liked his position at the Hall. He wasn't going to give it up for a penniless woman. But the two men did protect Elinor, letting the rest of you still believe it was Vanessa. David must have told Elinor that her name would be concealed, that she could leave with no embarrassment. She saw her chance. Elinor knew Vanessa would protect her. So Elinor deliberately misled Melissa and Deveraux."

Rosemary broke in. "I'll agree that most of the conversation by the lake—well, Elinor could very well have been talking about herself. But I remember the exact words in that one statement. She laughed and said, "Don't worry about me. I've been deserted before by Vanessa. When she married Sebastian.""

"Those were the words, Rosemary. What Elinor actually said was "Don't worry about me. I've been deserted before. By Vanessa when she married Sebastian." Sometimes we hear words the way we *think* they should sound.

"When Elinor left David that morning, she voiced the real threat on his life. She said, "You may regret this." Then she went ahead to make him regret it.

"David Mersey was Elinor's one chance at love. She had a strong, repressed nature. I would say for the balance of the day she was far from sane. Elinor was driven wild with jealousy, with hate. David had betrayed her, taken her body and discarded her. How would she have felt about Sebastian? He bought with his money and fame the one man she'd loved. Calmly, coldly, horribly, she plotted the murder."

"I can see all this," said Deveraux slowly. "But how did she get the drug into the wine? I know she had no chance, no chance at all."

"Very simple, she didn't. You were not drugged by the

wine. Elinor had plenty of time later that night to put a few drops in all the wine goblets but Sebastian's. Didn't any of you ever wonder at the speed with which the drug took effect? You'd hardly downed the wine before you were showing signs of the drug.

"I knew from the beginning there was something wrong with the time element. Melissa told me exactly how Elinor did it."

"She helped me with dinner," Melissa said dully. "It must have been in the coffee, the horrible coffee."

"Yes, the drug was in the coffee."

"I wasn't at dinner." Rosemary's voice was loud; it startled all of them. "I had no coffee and yet I was drugged too."

Forsythe looked at her. "You were indeed. Your aunt put on your dinner tray something Elinor knew you would drink—a glass of cream soda. Elinor knew all about your sweet tooth. She put the drug in the cream soda and you drank it."

"As soon as everyone was asleep, Elinor moved through the quiet house carrying out her plan. Deveraux was asleep in the drawing room, sprawled on an uncomfortable sofa. She took time to cover him, put a pillow under his head. Elinor did the most vicious deed I've ever heard of, but she was basically just what you thought her, a decent human being—a woman pushed to the breaking point, and she broke. The seed of violence erupted—one man died; the other was driven mad."

Forsythe placed his hand on Vanessa's shoulder. "Don't you think the time has come to break your silence. You can't shield your cousin any longer."

Vanessa tilted her head back and looked up at him. Her eyes were amused, but this time it was a bitter amusement. "I knew from the moment I saw you in Rome that you would never stop digging until you found Lin. I did my best to put you off the track, but it was no use. Very well, you've won.

"Lin was guilty. She killed David and did everything else the way you said. I didn't know at the time that David decided against her. It was something I couldn't have understood. I thought he had chosen Elinor. The night in the drawing room that I proposed the toast to the victor, I was speaking of my cousin. Sebastian told me to get out and take everything I'd brought, meaning Lin, with me. I touched David and told Sebastian I might take something else with me. I really thought David would come with Lin.

"The following morning when I saw Sebastian and David in the studio, I went wild. I believed that Sebastian had killed the boy to keep Elinor from having him. At the trial, I took the part of the villainess that I'm apparently cut out to be. I saw no purpose in exposing Lin to the pointing fingers and sneering mouths. The world believed that David was my lover, very well, let it.

"After the trial, I began to wonder. I was thinking more clearly. Many things started to bother me. Why had Lin taken David's death so calmly? I found out. My cousin was only too eager to confess to me. She wanted expiation. Lin was ready to go to the police. She had a ghastly conscience. Lin said she wanted to clear Sebastian so she could have peace. I talked her out of it."

"You talked her out of it." For the first time Elizabeth Pennell spoke. In her shadowy corner, her features were indistinct. "You could have solved the murder. Instead, you let me grow up believing my father did that terrible thing. Didn't you care?"

Vanessa shrugged. "About you or your relatives? No. I cared only for my cousin. I told Lin there was nothing to be gained. It would make no difference to Sebastian. Finally, I persuaded her to remain silent. She left me shortly afterward and went to Switzerland and her death."

Vanessa looked around, her eyes challenging. "Lin suffered for her crime—far more than any of you believe. Forsythe was right. She was a good woman. She paid."

The red-haired woman opened her handbag and removed a long envelope and a slim book bound in faded green. "After Lin's death, I was sent her personal effects. She didn't have many. A few clothes, some books, that was all. Among them was this book of poetry." She glanced around. "Are any of you familiar with Wilde's 'Ballad of Reading Gaol'?"

Several of them nodded. Vanessa turned the book over in her large shapely hands. "It's worn. There are marks on some pages that look very much like tear stains. There's one verse heavily underscored. Lin went through her own private hell."

She flipped the pages over and began to read. Her voice was level. A strange dignity about the woman held their attention.

> And there till Christ call forth the dead,
> In silence let him lie:
> No need to waste the foolish tear,
> Or heave the windy sigh:
> The man had killed the thing he loved,
> And so he had to die.

They sat quietly when her voice had stilled, all of them lost in their own thoughts.

Vanessa's voice broke the silence. "In this book was an envelope. The contents had been written two days before her death. It's a full confession, duly witnessed. Lin intended to clear Sebastian. If she'd lived, she would have."

Elizabeth was no longer in the shadow. She was on her feet facing Vanessa. "And you . . . you've held on to this more than twenty years while I thought— What kind of woman are you? Have you no pity?"

"Pity?" Vanessa raised a mocking brow. "Not for you. I don't think you require it. You have quite enough of your own. As for Rosemary and Melissa—yes, I now wish I'd turned the confession in. But it's too late."

Vanessa rose in one smooth motion, picked up her handbag and fur. Elizabeth backed away from her, her eyes blazing. Handing the envelope to Forsythe, Vanessa turned to Deveraux.

"It's too late for many things. One of my regrets will always be that I didn't notice you twenty-five years ago. Perhaps if I had, Richard, both our lives would have been different."

He struggled to his feet and extended one massive arm. "They say, Vanessa, that it's never too late. Shall we find out? I'll drive you back to London."

Vanessa took his arm and smiled up at him. Her amber eyes were luminous. Without a glance at anyone else, they left the room.

"Well!" Elizabeth was close to spitting. "Very pretty. And they lived happily ever after. What a grotesque pair!"

"Don't," said her aunt. "Please don't, Elizabeth. We've had enough of hate. Both Richard and Vanessa are unhappy people. They may have a chance for a life together."

Turning toward her own chair, Elizabeth gathered up her coat and handbag. She looked at Forsythe, quietly standing with the envelope in his hand.

"You'll know what to do with that. Thank you, Robert; you've been wonderful. May I see you later about your fee?"

"Of course. At your convenience. You can find me at my home in Sussex."

Melissa had risen. She put one hand on Elizabeth's arm. "Before you go home, my dear, will you come and see me? I'd so like to get to know you."

Elizabeth flinched away from her touch. She looked at her aunt. "I'm not a hypocrite. My father tossed me away like a piece of garbage and you allowed him to. I have no desire to know you. We're strangers now. Let it remain that way."

Nodding at Forsythe and Miss Sanderson, Elizabeth walked across the rose rug to the foyer. Forsythe returned the nod. Miss Sanderson didn't.

Rosemary hurried over to Melissa and put one arm around her waist. "The bitch! The cold, inhuman bitch!"

Behind the heavy glasses, her aunt's eyes looked damp, but her voice was firm. "No, Elizabeth's right. We're strangers. She'll never forgive me."

Melissa extended her hand to Forsythe. He clasped it in both of his. It was warm and dry; the skin felt like crushed rose petals. "There are no words. You've done so much for us. Sebastian's name will be cleared; Rosemary and Elizabeth will be free of fear. And you've given an old woman peace." She glanced around the big room. "This house, so many times I've been asked to sell it. I shall now. It knew happiness, laughter. Calvert Hall will have the chance to know these things again."

Melissa and Rosemary smiled their goodbyes at Forsythe before they turned away. Hennessy scrambled to open the door for them. He followed them through the foyer while Forsythe sank into a chair.

His feet parted, Horner had silently been watching. He spoke now. "I'm very much in your debt. You hit the nail on the head when you were talking about my wife's motive. For years, nightmares have haunted me. Remembering the type of girl she was, the way she felt about Calvert. Well—"

Forsythe finished for him. "You wondered whether Rosemary might have killed Mersey and Sebastian covered for her."

"Only with one part of my mind. I love my wife deeply but, damn it all, the way she felt about our boys, always watching them. I couldn't believe she worried about a great-uncle's violence. It seemed closer."

"More like a mother's violence?" Forsythe asked. "The

day I interviewed you in the shed, you knew Rosemary was listening, didn't you?"

Horner grinned. "She was listening, all right. Rosemary knows my beastly temper. She was trying to find out whether I was giving you a bad time. God, what suspicion can do. Say, how do you know all this?"

"I saw the fear in your eyes. You're not the sort to feel it for yourself."

Horner stuck out his hand, grasped Forsythe's warmly. "You'll never see it again." He turned to follow his wife and her aunt. Horner flung a parting remark over his shoulder. "Anytime you want anything, Forsythe, yell. I'll come running."

Pulling herself out of her chair, Miss Sanderson stretched. "I'm bushed. But that wraps it up." She glanced sideways at Forsythe. "I'm also starved. Do you suppose when we get back to the Inn, Bea might cut us a couple of sandwiches from that delicious pot roast we had tonight?"

Hennessy spoke behind them. "After what you did here, I'd guess that Bea will open her kitchen and make you a hot meal. You two go along now. I'll straighten up here."

Forsythe rose and wearily wandered the length of the room. He opened the doors that led to the studio. Miss Sanderson followed him and stood at his elbow. The moonlight was pouring through the glass walls.

"Do you notice, Robby, it feels warmer in here now?"

He grinned tiredly. "We have had a good fire going, you know."

"Not hot enough to penetrate this far."

"Now don't start talking about ghosts and auras again. These things don't exist. It's just that you're looking at this room in a different way. There never was anything waiting here."

She was watching the moonlight falling in silver ribbons across the stone floor. "I have a question, Robby. I know you're exhausted, but there's one thing you didn't explain and it's important."

"No more questions tonight. I know what you're thinking about. Later, old girl, much later."

Taking her elbow, he turned her away from the door. "Have I laid to rest all your ghosts and goblins for you?"

She took a last look at Sebastian Calvert's studio. "Perhaps," she said, "perhaps."

CHAPTER 12

The pond at the end of the garden no longer reflected blue August skies. A cold November wind driving icy rain before it turned the water into foaming steel gray.

Rain pounded against the long windows of Forsythe's study. Inside it was warm and cosy. The only sounds in the room were the scratch of a pen and the crackle of a wood fire. The russet cat sprawled full length on the carpet in front of the hearth, its eyes half closed.

Forsythe wrote steadily, copying in longhand from his father's closely written notes. When his secretary entered the room, he didn't look up.

"Visitors for you, Robby. Miss Pennell and a friend."

He pushed his work away. "Show them in, Sandy."

Elizabeth entered swiftly. Taking Forsythe's outstretched hand, she smiled at him. "I would imagine after all this time you thought I'd forgotten you."

"Not at all. You're looking well, Elizabeth."

She was. Her cherry wool suit was matched exactly by the tiny Robin Hood hat that perched on her dark hair. Under it, her eyes were bright and her expression vivacious.

Behind and to one side of her, a young girl waited. Forsythe looked at her with admiration. She was a beauty, gold and white with enormous blue eyes. Elizabeth made the introductions.

"This is my secretary, Darlee West. She joined me the first part of September and we've been making a tour of the continent.

Smiling at Elizabeth's companion, Forsythe said, "You must have had a chance to see many countries. Which did you prefer?"

Her voice was disappointing, high and nasal, with a midwestern twang. "I liked the south of France and some of Spain. We saw a bullfight in Madrid and—ugh!"

"No, they aren't very pleasant. Will you be seated?"

Darlee West daintily perched on the chair opposite the desk. Elizabeth stood behind it. Fishing in her handbag, she located and extended to Forsythe a small pink slip.

"Here is your fee, Robert; you said I could put my own value on your services."

He looked at the check. "But this is enormous. Far out of proportion to—"

"Not at all. I can well afford it, and you did do the impossible."

He placed it on his desk. "I must admit, Elizabeth, I'm surprised to see you in England. I thought you might have returned home to choose your trousseau and make plans for your wedding."

The beautiful little blonde swung around and looked up at her employer. "What's he talking about? What wedding?"

Placing one hand on the girl's shoulder, Elizabeth flicked her eyes across Forsythe's face. "You're mistaken, Robert; I have no intention of marrying."

"But when you came to see me, you said you were in love, that it was necessary to clear your father—"

He stopped abruptly. Elizabeth's large, spatulate hand was gently caressing the girl's shoulder. His face became cold and stern. "You deceived me."

Her eyes flashed with derision. "I didn't lie to you. All I said was that I'd fallen in love. You see, I am my father's daughter." She smiled. "Would you have taken the case if I'd told you my exact reason?"

"I damn well wouldn't have."

"There, you see? You're an old-fashioned man, Robert; it was necessary not to be too frank." She laughed, a brittle, tinkling sound. "Come now, don't look so forbidding. This is the latter part of the twentieth century, you know." She looked down at her secretary. "Come, Darlee; I have a feeling we're no longer welcome."

Forsythe had already pressed the button on the corner of his desk. Miss Sanderson opened the door as Darlee rose. His secretary waited.

"Show Miss Pennell and Miss West out, Sandy."

Stony-faced, he waited until the door closed behind them. He glanced down at the check. Then his lips began to quiver. He started to laugh, helplessly guffawing, holding on to the edge of the desk.

Miss Sanderson's voice broke across his laughter. "Share the joke, Robby."

She'd returned and was standing beside the desk staring at him. Helplessly he pointed to the pink slip. She picked it up, her eyes widening.

"Just when has a small fortune been funny?"

He struggled to control himself and sank breathless back into his chair.

"I think . . . I think we should have a drink to celebrate. Break out a bottle."

Her face still puzzled, she turned toward the door. He

called after her, "Bring in the files on the Calvert case, everything you have."

When Miss Sanderson nudged the door open, she was holding a large sheaf of manila folders with a tray precariously balanced on top.

Lifting off the tray, Forsythe proceeded to remove the cork from the green bottle. "Very good choice," he said, "champagne is suitable."

"You did say we were going to celebrate," she grunted, dumping the folders on the desk. "May I ask what the occasion is?"

"The emancipation of slaves," he said gaily, "the overthrow of tyranny and the death of a knight errant."

She accepted the brimming glass and looked suspiciously at him. "Are you sure you need this? I have a hunch you may have a snootful now."

He laughed and drank half his glass. "Sit down, Sandy, and prepare to take notes."

While she located her book and found a pen, Forsythe strode back and forth. The cat lifted a sleepy head and stared at him. He bent to pat it. "Now, make a list. I want my books crated"—he waved one hand expansively around him—"arrange to have the house closed. Meeks and his wife may as well stay on as caretakers. I want my chambers opened and cleaned. Get an ad in the *Times* for a couple of good clerks . . ."

Abigail Sanderson wasn't writing. She was staring at him, her mouth agape. He replenished his glass and waved the bottle at her. She shook her head. "One of us had better stay sober. Are you trying to tell me you intend to return to your practice?"

"That's exactly it, old girl. We're going back where both of us belong. We're going to begin living again. Close your mouth, Sandy; you're managing to look like an idiot."

Spots of color glowed high on her cheeks. "I can't believe it! What in the devil changed your mind?"

Forsythe picked up a manila envelope and began to lay the loose sheets of paper on the fire. "An old cliché, Sandy, but true. Elizabeth Pennell finally broke this camel's back. I saw her in her true colors and, at the same time, I saw myself." His eyes moved from the burning paper to Sandy's flushed face. "Have you any idea what was the real object of our earnest quest to prove the innocence of Sebastian Calvert?"

"You said Elizabeth was in love, wanted to—"

"In love, yes, much in love. In love with none other than her lovely young companion, Miss Darlee West." He groped for his glass and tipped it up.

Miss Sanderson held out her own glass. "On second thought, I'll have a touch more bubbly. I think I need it." She was smiling. After a moment her face became serious. "But this couldn't have changed your mind."

"It helped. I've been considering going back to work for some time. This did it. All that work, thought, struggle, just to promote the happiness of a full-blown lesbian. Sir Hilary was right and so, in a way, was the estimable Miss Pennell. This is the twentieth century and it's high time I came up to date. Now is the time to ask your question, Sandy, the one you wanted answered that night in Calvert Hall."

She twirled the stem of her goblet. "Very well. I've had a tough time trying not to force an answer from you. Your reasoning was sound. Elinor Atlin killed David Mersey. Her confession clinched it. But—if she was the murderess—who the devil took a shot at you? The only person who tried to protect Elinor was Vanessa Calvert. And Vanessa was in Rome. She might have hired a killer to stop you, but I can't believe it. I feel Vanessa would do her own killing. Anyway, a professional assassin would have been thorough. I can't see one giving up after a solitary try."

"Sound reasoning, Sandy. I believed that one of our suspects was out to finish me off until I knew definitely the identity of Mersey's killer. Then I suddenly realized who my assailant had been. Think, Sandy, what else had I done the day that I was nicked?"

For a moment, there was only the sound of the soft tapping of Miss Sanderson's nail against her tooth. "Well," she softly, "we worked through the forenoon in our suite. You had lunch with Richard Deveraux and came back to the hotel. Then you went out to meet Elizabeth. On your way back the shot was fired." She stared at him. "Not Elizabeth."

"Hardly. No possible reason why she'd want her sleuth dead. No, I met someone else that evening. You must have a mental block about her. You should remember."

"I certainly should. I loathe her. Virginia, Virginia Telser."

"Now Mrs. Douglas Graham. Yes, little Virginia. I never discussed our meeting with you. The old magic was gone. The moment I saw her I knew she was merely another man's wife. Whatever I'd felt for her was over. I suppose a woman always knows. Another thing I know now is that Virginia was guilty. She blew Frank Telser's brains out and planted fake evidence to blame a prowler—"

"I always knew *that*. You would have too if you'd been able to think clearly. The woman was besotted with Graham. She'd have done anything to get him."

"And she'll do anything to keep him. I looked dangerous to her. She was afraid I'd blow her paradise to pieces. So Virginia followed me to the Monument, then to the hotel, and tried to ensure her safety by killing me." He ripped some pages out viciously and threw them on the flames. "The poor fool, she didn't understand she had my word. No matter how I felt about her, I'd have kept it." The cat moved; it was rubbing against his knee. One of his hands brushed its bright, thick fur.

"What Virginia doesn't know is that I have some insurance myself. Murdering me would only have exposed her. I took a statement from Albert Jennings that will stand up in court. It's in my safety box in London, and would have been opened after my death."

His secretary leaned forward. "What will happen to you? In a way you've been concealing evidence."

"I'll have my fingers rapped. But it was privileged information. Virginia is the one they'll roast. The case will either be reopened or they'll try her on a charge of bribing a key witness. Either way, she'll be out of circulation for a long time."

"Her son, Robby, how do you feel about him?"

"Badly," Forsythe admitted. "But my promise has been canceled out. Now that Virginia has tried to kill me once, she may have another go. I don't really fancy setting myself up for target practice."

Miss Sanderson looked dazed. "I'm finding it hard to believe." Her eyes sharpened. "What was that about the death of a knight errant and Sir Hilary?"

"He compared me to Don Quixote. As usual, Sir Hilary was brutally accurate. I can hardly see Sir Lancelot riding out to battle wearing the colors I did—one gallant banner for a cold-blooded murderess, the other for a lesbian."

"You must remember, Robby, that your last ride did a great deal of good for a nice group of people. What about Melissa Calvert and Rosemary?"

"Agreed. But the good was purely coincidental. No, Robert Forsythe has ridden that trail for the last time. The next time we don armor, Sandy, it will be in a court of law, for someone who really needs our help." He rose from the hearth. "Finish burning these, will you? I feel restless. I'm going for a walk before tea."

Picking up the check, she held it delicately by one corner between her thumb and forefinger. "What about this?"

"Burn it—" he stopped abruptly. "On second thought, that sounds like the old Robert Forsythe. No, deposit it in our business account. We've earned it and, as Elizabeth said, she can afford it." He grinned at his secretary. "It may help provide funds for someone who can't afford our services."

Flinging open the window, he stepped over the sill. She watched him as he strode across the wet turf. His shoulders moved easily and his step was brisk and young.

With a smile, she turned to the hearth. Kneeling in front of the fire, she laid the rest of the papers on the flames. They flared up and burned briskly. In a short time all that remained of the Calvert case was gray ashes.